Étienne M. Faillon

The Christian Heroine of Canada

Life of Miss Le Ber

Étienne M. Faillon

The Christian Heroine of Canada
Life of Miss Le Ber

ISBN/EAN: 9783337194550

Printed in Europe, USA, Canada, Australia, Japan

Cover: Foto ©Andreas Hilbeck / pixelio.de

More available books at **www.hansebooks.com**

THE

CHRISTIAN HEROINE

OF

CANADA;

OR,

LIFE OF MISS LE BER.

Translated from the French.

Montreal:

PRINTED BY JOHN LOVELL.

———

1861.

INTRODUCTION.

A desire of extending the knowledge of
Catholicity, was the principal motive that
induced the kings of France, Francis I,
Henry IV, and Louis XIII, to establish a
French colony in Canada ; and this intention
is formally expressed in their royal mandates.
Even Lescarbot, who, at that time, was generally known not to be a great practical catholic,
and consequently cannot be accused of partiality towards our Religion, was so struck with the
pure and disinterested intention that directed
these princes, that he rendered the following testimony in their favour : " Our kings, in
" taking an active part in these discoveries,
" had a different end in view from that which
" guided our neighbours (the English and
" Dutch), for I see by their letters, that they
" sought only the glory of God, and the pro-

" gress of the Christian religion, indepen-
" dently of any personal advantage."

Jacques Cartier, who, in obedience to an
order from Francis I, braved the perils of the
deep in these unknown regions, had no other
ambition than the hope of affording an asylum
to the Catholic Church, then so violently persecuted in Europe by the growing protestant
heresy.

In dedicating the memoirs of his second
voyage to this monarch, he says: " As the
" sun, in his daily revolution round the earth,
" imparts both light and heat to the entire
" globe; so has it pleased God, in his infinite
" goodness, that all human beings should be
" enlightened by our Holy Faith, which, for-
" merly sown and planted in the Holy Land,
" has since been brought to us; and finally,
" like the orb of day, will pass from Europe
" to the far west.   And as the sun, in his daily
" course, is often eclipsed and then suddenly
" bursts forth with more dazzling brilliancy;
" thus also our Holy Faith has been persecuted
" by false legislators, and calumniated by their
" followers, such as the Lutherans of the pres-
" ent day; and it has always been in these
" trying circumstances that its divine strength
" has been miraculously proved.   This is partly
" owing to the fact that Christian princes, those

" pillars of the Catholic church, act in direct
" opposition to the children of Satan, and stren-
" uously endeavour to increase and strengthen
" the Faith. Thus, the king of Spain proved
" his devotedness to the church, by ordering
" expeditions for the discovery of New Spain
" and other countries previously unknown.
" In this navigation, undertaken in compliance
" with your royal command, to discover west
" ern climes unknown to you and to us; you
" can see (by this report) the fertility of these
" lands, the number of people that inhabit
" them, their benevolence and mildness, as
" well as the riches of the magnificent river
" which flows in this country. These advan-
" tages give rise to well-founded anticipations
" relative to the progress of our Holy Faith
" in this country."

This motive of apostolic zeal, which had
brought Jacques Cartier so far as the Island of
Montreal, was manifested still more a century
later, by giving rise to the foundation of a
Catholic colony. The disinterested associates
who devoted themselves to this remarkable
undertaking, sought only the honor of diffusing
the light of the Gospel in this island. Their
desire, expressed in their own words, was:
" To celebrate God's praises in a desert where
" the name of Jesus Christ had never yet

" been pronounced, and which, until that date,
" had been the abode of evil spirits." They
intended to build a city, which might become
the bulwark of the Catholic church in that
part of the new world ; and as Mary's name
has ever been the terror of heretics and the
banner of the true children of the Church,
they wished that this infant city should be
called Ville Marie, and be most specially consecrated to this mighty sovereign, the invincible shield of the true Faith. Their aim was
also the honour of Jesus, Mary, and Joseph :
for which reason they wished to establish three
religious communities, each consecrated to one
of these august persons ; but, whose separate
efforts would have one common end ; namely,
the formation and support of this new Church.

The following lines are an extract from the
prospectus of colonisation : " the associates,
" whose only reliance is in God's infinite good-
" ness, hope that a new Christian society shall
" soon arise, which by its purity and charity
" will be a perfect copy of the primitive church."

The success that crowned these efforts is too
well known to mention it at present. We shall
not here dwell on the zeal of these first colonists
who sundered all ties of home and kindred, to
carry out their pious design, nor on the transports of holy joy manifested when first they set

foot on Mary's special domain, and the hymns
of grateful praise which burst forth on that
occasion ; nor shall we call to mind the fervour
with which they assisted at the adorable sacrifice of the Mass, the day after their arrival ;
nor that profound religious feeling which induced them to expose the Blessed Sacrament for
public worship during the entire day, the more
openly to acknowledge by this august ceremony
that Jesus Christ Himself took possession of the
land ; and in order that succeeding generations
should learn that this new establishment had
been undertaken with the sole desire of promoting God's glory and the extension of his kingdom on earth.

Our object here is to remark, that, as the
Catholic church has been commissioned from
above to lead men to God, it should, as the ark,
out of which there is no salvation, give striking
proofs of its divine mission ; and Ville Marie
was destined to render this testimony throughout the whole extent of North America.   The
true church has certain marks by which it is
known : Unity of faith and government is one
of its peculiar characteristics, universality
extending its doctrines throughout all parts of
the inhabited world, and its apostolical mission
by which its origin can be traced to the time of
the Apostles ; to these qualities a fourth and

more striking one can be added: the sanctity of its members as well as of its doctrines. If, according to Jesus Christ, the church can be compared to a field wherein cockle has been sown, there will always be good grain among it: that is, not only will righteous souls be ever found in its midst; but, persons eminent for sanctity, whose heroic virtues, and sometimes whose miracles will astonish the most incredulous, thus giving palpable proofs of the truth of the Catholic church, the only one founded by Jesus Christ; and proving that God's divine spirit directs and guides it in all things.

The examples given by several colonists of New France have confirmed this doctrine. They resembled the primitive Christians by their touching piety, their mutual generosity and charity; their unconquerable courage, their patience and mildness in the midst of the frightful torments which they endured in defence of that Faith. All these admirable traits of virtue would furnish sufficient materials for a considerable work,—but this is not our aim: we seek to make known the life of a Christian virgin, one whose heroic fervour is another proof of the divine mission of Catholicity in these countries. Miss Le Ber, such is our heroine's name, was the daughter of one of the first colonists whom religious zeal had led to the establishment of Ville Marie.

Miss Le Ber renewed in the land of her birth the fervour of the anchorites of the primitive Church. During thirty-five years she lived separated from the world, leading a life that required miraculous intervention to prevent the exhaustion of natural strength.

The Catholic church alone can record such astonishing facts, and dissenting sects have never shewn, nor ever shall possess similar examples.

Miss Le Ber's reclusion is a fact of public notoriety throughout Canada; the recollection has been transmitted to us along with the greatest veneration for her. It can be proved at the present time, by various contemporary monuments both public and autographical, such as acts of donations, and other acts found at the prothonotary's office, legally authorised by notaries and signed by the pious recluse, at the entrance of her cell.

This fact is also mentioned by several writers of that period, as eliciting general admiration: it is spoken of by mother Juchereau, in her history of the Hotel-Dieu of Quebec; by sister Morin, in her annals of the Hotel-Dieu of Ville Marie; by sister Bourgeoys, in her memoirs; by Mr. de Belmont, who wrote the

holy solitary's life ; by Mr. de Bacqueville de
la Potherie, in his history of North America.
A quotation from the latter will serve as an
introduction to Miss Le Ber's life : " It would
" be impossible for me not to allude to a most
" striking example of extraordinary virtue
" given by a young lady now residing with the
" Sisters of the Congregation of Notre Dame.

" Miss Le Ber, daughter of the richest mer-
" chant in Canada, although she had always
" led a most retired life in her own home ; yet
" thinking that God called her to one more
" secluded, withdrew seven or eight years ago,
" from her father's house, and went to the Sis-
" ters of the Congregation of Notre Dame.
" Her dwelling there is a small apartment sur-
" rounded by walls, having but one window
" opening on the chapel, and a small aperture
" at her door, through which she receives her
" food.   Her spiritual director is Mr. Ségue-
" not of the Seminary of Saint Sulpice.   Al-
" though she devotes several hours each day
" to meditation, she nevertheless finds time for
" ornamental work, which she bestows on the
" different communities.   The floor is her only
" couch, and her only visitors are her director
" and her father ; the latter she sees but once
" or twice a year.   Notwithstanding her isola-
" tion from her fellow-creatures, she is mild

" and docile : this solitary life seems to have
" become natural to her."

This holy recluse's life was destined by God
not only as a striking proof in favour of the
Catholic church ; but the Almighty also intended
that it should be as a bright luminary, whose
mild rays would gladden and enliven all true
children of the Church ; for Miss Le Ber was
proposed to all the faithful as a touching model
of the purest Christian virtues, and her fervour
induced many young persons to consecrate
themselves wholly to his service, while a still
greater number were led to the practice of
Christian perfection in the world.

We will add that her life will offer to all
Christian families admirable examples of virtue,
most worthy of imitation. The family Le Ber
presents a perfect copy of the Holy Family,
Jesus, Mary and Joseph, whom the early colonists were so desirous of imitating. Not only
will children find in Miss Le Ber an amiable
and touching model, but fathers and mothers
will also find in the happy union effected by
Mr. and Mrs. Le Ber, examples of the most
loving and devoted affection towards their
children, united to the greatest fidelity to God,
the supreme Father of all.

This life will be divided into four books.
The first, will treat of Miss Le Ber's early

years, until she left the boarding school; and here she will be held forth as a model of perfection to all school-girls. The second, will embrace the time which elapsed from the termination of her education until her withdrawal from the world, and her retirement in the convent of the Congregation of Notre Dame; wherein she will be presented to all young persons desirous of sanctifying themselves in the world, as a model of a perfect life. The third, will make known her devotion to Jesus Christ in the adorable Sacrament of the altar, and the practices by which she evinced her love. The fourth, will prove her devotion towards the Blessed Virgin, and her holy death. In these last two books, she will serve as a model of truly magnanimous virtue to all Religious; and generally to persons in all states of life.

We beg that God, who, in His divine mercy, formerly gave such efficacy to this virgin's heroic examples of virtue, may bless this work and bless those who read it. May the recital of this holy life produce in all hearts the most signal effects of grace, by detaching them more and more from all creatures and themselves, in order to unite them more closely to God.

BOOK FIRST.

MISS LE BER'S CHILDHOOD.—HER SOJOURN AT
THE URSULINE CONVENT IN QUEBEC.

CHAPTER I.

MISS LE BER'S FAMILY.—HER BIRTH.—HER
BAPTISM.—HER EARLY TRAINING.

JANE LE BER, whose life we write, had the happiness of belonging to one of the most virtuous families with which God has endowed Canada. Her father, James Le Ber, a native of Pistre in the diocese of Rouen, having devoted his services to the foundation of Ville Marie, never after deviated from the noble disinterestedness which had led him to sever all ties of home and kindred. God, to reward him, even in this life, gave the *hundred fold* promised in Scripture to those who leave all for His love.

B

Besides that peace of heart which is the greatest
benefit man can enjoy here below, Mr. Le Ber
found in his voluntary sacrifice, the acquisition
even of those temporal advantages he seemed to
have renounced, by taking part in all the perils
and privations of that colonisation. God's blessing attended all his commercial enterprises, and he
soon became the richest merchant in Canada, and
at the same time one of the most esteemed men of
New France. His benevolence towards the poor,
his strict probity in business, the open profession
of the principles of faith and of Christian morality;
and his disinterested zeal for the public good,—
won for him golden opinions from his fellow-citizens, confidence from the Governor; and most
particular marks of the Monarch's esteem, who
deigned to honour him and his descendants with
the prerogatives then attached to nobility.*

---

* Louis XIV. ennobled Mr. Le Ber's family by mandates written in November 1696; and Louis XV. sus-
tained their nobility, by an order of the 9th of March,
1717. Mr. Le Ber took the title of Le Ber de Saint
Paul, from the Island, of which he possessed the two-
thirds. Although these two-thirds were situated at
both extremities of the island, they formed but one fief;
the other third belonged to Claude de Robutel de Saint
André. His son, Zacharias de Robutel, exchanged the
two-thirds of his share with the Nuns of the Congregation de Notre Dame; and the following year his sister,
Anne de Robutel, sold the remaining part of the third
to them; so that they thus acquired one-third of Saint
Paul's island, and became sole possessors of it in 1769.

The most precious benefit conferred on Mr. Le
Ber was his union with Jane Lemoyne, whose
brother Charles received some time afterwards the
title of Baron of Longueuil.   This young lady's
virtue and high moral sentiments rendered her
truly worthy of him; and their united efforts
tended to inspire their children with love and
veneration for the maxims of the Gospel.   Their
daughter, whose life we write, was born at Ville
Marie on the 4th of January, 1662; and was baptized the same day by Mr. Gabriel Souart, in the
parish church.   This favoured child, destined one
day to become, by her sanctity and heroism, the
honour and glory of her country, was worthy of
being presented to God at the baptismal font by
the two most distinguished persons to whom the
colony was indebted, both for its establishment and
its preservation.   Her godfather was Mr. Paul de
Chomedey de Maisonneuve, sent by the proprietors
of the island of Montreal as governor thereof, and
who had been instrumental in establishing the
colony; her godmother was Miss Mance, foundress and first administratrix of the Hôtel-Dieu;
who also took an active part in all that regarded
the welfare of Ville Marie, as may be seen in her
life.

When Miss Mance presented the child for baptism, she gave her, her own name, Jane; and our
heroine bore it ever afterwards.   It would not be
inconsistent on our part here to remark that a wise
and religious spirit then directed parents in the

choice of patron saints for their children. Persons
of all ranks esteemed it an honor to bear the names
of those sanctified souls who had been most favoured
and loved by our Divine Lord or His Immaculate
Mother.   They preferred those of the Apostles, or
of other personages who were connected with the
Holy Family, and who, on this account, are most
specially honoured by the Church.   Mr. de Maisonneuve, the descendant of a noble family of
Champagne, had received the name of Paul; Miss
Mance, who was also of honourable extraction, and
highly honoured by the Queen Regent, mother of
Louis XIV., and by several ladies of the court,
was called Jane; and the Queen, who gave her
such marks of consideration, gloried in bearing
the name of Anne, it being that of the Blessed
Virgin's mother.*

---

* Now-a-days, parents follow a very different line of
conduct. Very many, although far from being distinguished by birth, talents, or fortune, seem ashamed to
bestow on their children the names of venerated and
illustrious saints. If at times they apparently conform
to the desire of the Church so far as to give them a
saint's name, a vain wish of distinguishing themselves
induces them also to give their children appellations
almost unheard of, and sometimes most ridiculous.
They hope, that, by such means, they may place themselves above others. They do not consider that, in
acting thus, they mingle with the most vulgar, who
alone are deluded by this false pride. Although they
succeed in exciting remarks, they differ from the most
honorable portion of society, who in France at the
present time still continue to give their children names
which some classes consider beneath them.

.

As the first glimmering of reason became per-
ceptible in our youthful Jane, the happy effects of
baptismal grace were also manifested. This was
owing to the exertions of her pious mother, who
fulfilled all the obligations of her position, never
neglecting an opportunity of developing her child's
mind, and of strengthening regenerating grace.
In order to prepare her for the practices of Christian virtue, it was her desire that instruction should
precede the use of reason. To procure this, she
endeavoured to render her familiar with the life of
Jesus Christ, even when she was yet at so tender
an age that her intellect could not understand
these lessons, nor her memory retain them. Her
maternal assiduity was crowned with success, and
this worthy mother was richly rewarded on beholding, later, her child's inclinations directed, as if by
instinct, from the very dawn of reason, towards
God; and she rejoiced to see the first affections of
her tender heart consecrated to the love of her
Creator.

This child of predilection had scarcely attained
her sixth year when she paid daily visits to her
godmother, Miss Mance, and the Hospital Nuns.
Our little Jane's great delight was to interrogate
the Sisters concerning our Saviour, and the mysteries of His life. That of the Holy Childhood
seemed the most attractive to her young mind, and
she always spoke of it with extraordinary sentiments of esteem and love. These inclinations in
one so young astonished Miss Mance. She never

wearied admiring the precocious wisdom of her
reflections, the correctness and penetration of her
judgment, accompanied by an insatiable thirst for
knowing God's motives in creating everything that
struck her.   On beholding any thing new, she
always inquired for what particular end God had
created it.

Mrs. Le Ber having succeeded in forming her
daughter's heart to the practice of Christian virtues, knew well that, although Baptism makes us
children of God, it does not destroy the vicious inclinations we bring into the world with us; and
that a germ of pride, a love of sensual pleasure,
and an inordinate attachment to worldly goods, are
found in the purest hearts.   She was also aware
that Jesus Christ sends his Holy Spirit to reside
in our souls, by the Sacrament of Baptism, to assist us in triumphing over these natural propensi-
ties, and to inspire us with sentiments of humility,
of mortification, and of detachment from all things
earthly, and to enable us to lead a life conformable
to His.   Being thoroughly impressed with the idea
that the chief duty imposed upon parents is to
strengthen the sentiments of Jesus Christ in their
children's minds, and that this task devolves particularly upon Christian mothers, whom Divine
providence has appointed to attend to the first
training, Mrs. Le Ber spared no means of implant-
ing the truths of our holy religion in our heroine's
heart, and from the child's infancy neglected no
occasion that could tend to inspire her with an

aversion to vanity, a vice which is so directly opposed to a true Christian spirit, and so fruitful in innumerable evils. Although this virtuous mother conformed to all the exigencies of her position, and always dressed her daughter in a suitable manner, she endeavoured to impress her with the idea that she was to use such things without attaching her heart to them, thereby preventing the evil effects attendant upon an inordinate love of dress.

Our heroine manifested great docility, and from an early period proved that she would one day become a perfect model of all the virtues which should adorn a Christian virgin. More certain proofs of solid virtue, a greater love of prayer, more modesty in deportment, purer charity towards equals, and greater compassion for the afflicted, had perhaps never before been seen in one so young; such was the result of the Christian education she had received from her mother.

If Mrs. Le Ber's example is followed by some Christian mothers of the present day, on the other hand must we not acknowledge that many mothers, far from inspiring their children with love for the maxims of the gospel, which is one of their most important obligations, seek to fill their young minds with a love of pomp and vanity; thus setting aside the engagements contracted at baptism.

At the present day mothers often exhaust all their resources on a child's apparel, and that even when the child can scarcely stand without assistance, then delight in praising and admiring it,

and endeavour by all available means to add to its
appearance and to exaggerate its beauty. The expression of excessive joy which beams in their
parents' looks and countenances, the animated language, the strong gestures they use to express their
satisfaction, and many other demonstrations, make
a deeper impression upon children's hearts than is
generally believed; they lead them to vanity and
to a boundless esteem of self. This is observed in
the pleasing positions they endeavour to assume,
in their general demeanour, and in all their little
actions, which sometimes indicate great haughtiness,—some even get so proud as to look down
upon other children on whom praise is not bestowed
or whose apparel is less costly.

By such perfidious insinuations, the power and
charms of a mother's love are directed towards a
wrong end, when they ought to be used to prepare
young hearts for the practice of the virtues of
Faith, Hope, and Charity, virtues which they received at baptism. They on the contrary, contribute to weaken those holy inclinations; and before
the dawn of reason, the evil effects of such training are perceived by the pride, haughtiness, and
disdain which young children manifest.

When the light of faith does not direct the
earliest formation of the mind, such evil consequences must always follow. But the efforts of
maternal kindness, enlightened by wisdom, will be
seen to have produced very different results in our
heroine.

CHAPTER II.

MISS LE BER ENTERS THE URSULINE CONVENT IN QUEBEC. HER MORTIFICATION. HER POLITENESS. HER CHARITY TOWARD HER COMPANIONS.

Although the *Memoirs* that have been transmitted to us concerning Miss Le Ber, do not inform us that the venerable sister Bourgeoys, foundress of the Congregation of Notre Dame, took any part in her first education, it is most probable that her virtuous mother received great assistance from this estimable person in forming her child's heart to virtue, and in instructing her in the rudiments of profane science. This opinion is founded upon the fact that sister Bourgeoys bestowed the same attention upon all the little girls of Ville Marie; and parents of all classes esteemed her so highly, that they were happy to place their children under her care; so that they too might be sharers in the special blessings which attended her devoted endeavours.

When Miss Le Ber had attained her eighth year, sister Bourgeoys, being unable to meet the educational wants of the country, went to France to obtain assistance which could not be had in Canada; at the same time she solicited letters patent to insure the future success of her institution. During two years the colony was thus deprived of the presence of the holy foundress. It was probably during this interval that Mrs. Le Ber placed her daughter at the Ursuline Convent in Quebec. This devoted mother, aware that her daughter would receive the greatest care, and that her mind would be properly trained, hesitated not to part with her and send her 60 leagues from Ville Marie: hers was truly Christian tenderness; God's will being her law, she wavered not when thoroughly convinced that her child's welfare demanded this sacrifice. Miss Le Ber was therefore sent to the Ursuline Convent in Quebec.

If a tree can be judged by the fruit it bears, and the ability of teachers by the pupils whose minds they form, the greatest eulogium which can be pronounced on the Ursulines' manner of training children, is the fact that they were chosen by an All-wise Providence to form the mind and heart of this wonderful child, who afterwards became the prodigy of her age, and the most perfect model that can be offered to young persons in Canada. The result proved that God had so ordained things, in order to bring this child's virtue to light, and to show what blessings he had showered upon her;

us also to impress her teachers and her companions with a profound idea of her virtue.

Forty years later the Ursulines rendered the following testimony in her favour : " Miss Le Ber,
" while a boarder in our institution, gave from her
" earliest youth instances of sublime acts of virtue,
" far beyond her age. She manifested a particular
" distaste, or rather a decided horror, of vanity and
" of all wordly grandeur : having a singular love of
" solitude and silence, a marked inclination for an
" interior life ; and mental prayer seemed to be
" her favorite exercise. She was most submissive
" and respectful towards her teachers. Such were
" the qualities we remarked in her. Some in-
" stances will give an insight into her general con-
" duct. Several persons in Quebec, acquainted
" with Miss Le Ber, were in the habit of sending
" her various objects of amusement, and some
" delicacies of which children are generally so
" fond ; on such occasions she would apologize
" politely for declining to accept them, for her spirit
" of mortification would not allow her to indulge in
" any sensuality, but prompted her to use all avail-
" able means to mortify her inclinations."

What consummate virtue in such a tender age ! what a perfect model for all school girls ! What a difference between her and those delicate or rather sensual children, who ask for various delicacies, and who always receive them with such unbecoming de- monstrations of joy : Miss Le Ber refuses those that are offered to her. This Christian conduct proves how she had mortified every propensity to sensuality. All who saw her were edified and profoundly touched by such extraordinary mortification.

Notwithstanding her strong love of mortification, it never led her to neglect any duty imposed by custom or Christian charity. When she thought that a refusal of any offering would displease those who presented it to her, she accepted it willingly, preferring self mortification and the sacrifice of a legitimate and even holy desire, rather than disoblige the persons who bestowed so much kindness and attention upon her. Such enlightened condescension on the part of our heroine proved that her love of mortification, was a certain mark of solid virtue, and not the effect of caprice, as is the case with some children who mould devotion to suit their fancy.

Her teachers conclude by these words : " When " politeness prompted her to accept various articles " and delicacies which were offered to her, it was " for the purpose of distributing them among those " of her companions whom they might please." By this generous sacrifice she was enabled to practise charity towards others, without diminishing her love of mortification.

Though we sometimes meet children who are so selfish as not to share with any of their companions the delicacies which are given them, and others who will not allow their playmates to use any of their toys, yet we must acknowledge that a greater number are induced by kindness or by virtue to make others partakers in their enjoyments: but an example of heroic virtue which had perhaps never before been seen, was given by Miss Le Ber, who deprived herself so voluntarily of all such enjoyments to impart them to her companions. This cannot surprise us when we are reminded that God destined this child of predilection, to be a model of mildness and mortification for all school girls.

CHAPTER III.

MISS LE BER PROVES BY HER SIMPLICITY IN
CHOOSING THE PLAINEST ARTICLES, HER
HORROR OF VANITY; AND GIVES TO HER
COMPANIONS EXAMPLES OF ADMIRABLE
HUMILITY.

As Miss Le Ber was perfectly detached from
self, she never endeavoured to gain the esteem of
those who surrounded her; and thus differed from
the generality of children, who aim at being admired, and, the better to ensure success, generally
choose articles that are remarkable for their beauty
and brilliancy, as if these objects would give them
any personal merit. Our heroine, animated by a
very different spirit, not only avoided sensuality,
but also sought great simplicity, and every object
destined for her use was first carefully examined:
if it was merely ornamental, and likely to excite
thoughts of vanity, she begged to be excused
from accepting it, unless politeness or obedience
obliged her to do so; and even then she would

find means of satisfying her simplicity, as the following instance will prove.

Knowing that idleness is the mother of all vices, she particularly avoided it. Among other acquirements she had begun to make lace work: A lady offered her a cushion to use for this sort of work; it was ornamented with various ribbons which gave it a gaudy appearance. Miss Le Ber remarked it, her first impulse was to refuse it, and she politely apologized to the giver for so doing. Seeing however that the lady persisted, and fearing that a reiterated refusal might wound the generous donor's feelings, our heroine consented to accept the cushion. As soon as she was free she unfastened all the ornaments, and, although they were valuable, she was about to throw them into the fire, when one of her teachers noticed her and prevented the execution of her design.

She was reprimanded for this; the cushion was again trimmed in its primitive style, and she was obliged to use it as the lady had given it to her. Miss Le Ber willingly submitted to her mistresses, for her obedience was so perfect that it alone guided her mortifications; but this child's strong Christian spirit was proved by the fact, that she acted in such direct opposition to her own inclination when obliged to use this cushion, that she bedewed it with her tears. It was not caprice that made them flow, nor sorrow, because she was sacrificing her own will, as is generally the case when children are contradicted. The Ursulines, struck with the purity of the motives which caused such abundant tears to flow, and fearing that the progress of grace might be impeded if they persisted, allowed her to untrim the cushion, and to use it in its simplest form.

The Ursulines thus conclude their eulogium: " We always admired such disdain and disgust for " all trifles, at an age when most children are "generally so anxious to possess them. It was " evident that, even at that early age, Miss Le Ber " judged of every thing by the light of faith; and " finding that all useless ornaments were connected " with the world which Jesus Christ had con- " demned, her tender piety led her to renounce " interiorly those pomps and vanities which all " Christians renounce in Baptism."

This Christian conduct should awaken feelings of sorrow and confusion within the breasts of many children. Some who are never content with what their condition allows them, endeavour to acquire the most expensive and showy articles. Others who are deprived of such things, envy those children who possess them; and these in their turn delight in the possession of them, and sometimes despise their companions who are less favored by fortune.

Miss Le Ber was one of the most distinguished pupils in the Ursuline Convent. This was owing to the honorable position her parents held, to the natural abilities which she manifested, to her easy and graceful manner of speaking, to the success she obtained in her studies, and in the various styles of needlework which were then taught. All these advantages seemed to distinguish her from the majority of her companions, and to give her a right to some mark of distinction; yet a more modest and retiring young person could not be met with; her only aim was to remain unknown.

The testimony given by her teachers will be read with edification. "On many occasions she " manifested her love of solitude and retirement. " It is customary for our pupils about Christmas " time, and sometimes at other festivals, to learn " pastorals or other pious dialogues, to cultivate " and usefully adorn the memory, and to accus- " tom them to speak naturally and gracefully " Miss Le Ber always did so in a most becoming " manner; but consented to do it very unwillingly, " as it exposed her to attract attention and to re- " ceive applause. To avoid this, her humility " afforded her means of attracting as little atten- " tion as possible."

"In these dialogues, each pupil receives a part. " Care is taken, in distributing these parts, to " suit them as closely as possible to the character " and inclination of the pupil. Although Miss " Le Ber liked retirement, she never refused to " take part in these exercises with her companions, " because she disliked dispensations and peculiari- " ties, but, though well calculated to play the most " prominent parts, she always preferred the most " insignificant, where little capacity was required,

" and which even seemed to draw disdain upon
" the actor."

Such is the infallible mark of consummate virtue. If a naturally timid child, with a poor
memory, preferred inferior parts, one could easily
account for this, since a fear of exposing her inca-
pacity might induce her to do so ; but true humility
alone could lead a talented young girl, whose
graceful elocution would win great applause,
to select an insignificant part which placed her
beneath her companions. What a contrast between
Miss Le Ber's feelings and inclinations and those
of some young persons who are placed in similar
circumstances !

This holy child here finds means of amusing
and edifying her companions, and also of giving an
additional proof of her love for God, while others
are led to neglect their religious duties, and sometimes even to commit sin by the thought of vanity
and self-complacency to which success in these rep-
resentations may give rise. It is true that such
children neglect no means of acting their parts
properly ; and by so doing, they certainly accomplish a duty, and deserve approbation ; but instead
of aiming at God's greater glory and conformity
to His divine will which is made known to them
by their teachers, or endeavouring to instruct
others, alas ! no such christian motive guides them :
the sole stimulant of all their efforts is the ambi-
tious desire of gaining applause, and of impressing

all present with a great idea of their personal consequence.

When thus actuated by pride, these children unfortunately forget that they are Christians, for all true Christians ever endeavour to imitate Jesus Christ and to practice the evangelical maxim: " Learn of me, because I am meek and humble of heart." Miss Le Ber, however, endeavoured to model her conduct on that of her divine Master. It was in imitation of Jesus, who fled when the multitude wished to proclaim him king, that Miss Le Ber preferred insignificant parts to more prominent ones, so that she too might avoid public notice and lead a retired life.

Miss Le Ber's ardent love for her divine Master also gave rise to her great desire of imitating Him. All persons willingly resemble those who have gained their affections, and if our hearts were inflamed with the ardent love which burned in Miss Le Ber's, our only aim would be to follow her example by endeavouring to imitate our divine Lord. The Ursulines add the following edifying trait: " On one occasion, when parts were distri-" buted among the pupils, Miss Le Ber's tender " love of our Lord, and her desire of resembling " Him, betrayed her humility and gave a most " striking proof of the admirable dispositions of " her heart. We wished to represent the adoration " of the shepherds at the crib. One of the teach-" ers asked Miss Le Ber whom she wished to " represent. She replied, without the slightest

" hesitation, ' The infant Jesus.' ' Your choice
" is certainly not bad,' was the reply, ' but what
" induces you to make it?' ' The holy child
" neither speaks nor moves, and my desire is to
" imitate Him in all things.' Such was her edify-
" ing answer."

CHAPTER IV.

MISS LE BER'S FIDELITY TO SILENCE WHEN
PRESCRIBED BY THE RULE.—HER CONSTANT
RECOLLECTION OF THE DIVINE PRESENCE.
—HER LOVE FOR MEDITATION.

Miss Le Ber could be held forth to all her
schoolmates as a model of perfect conformity to all
the rules of the institution. None could be compared to her for fidelity in observing silence at the
hours when the rule prescribed it. It is true that
this regulation, which is so repugnant to some
children, was most pleasing to her. The result of
her constant endeavours was to discipline all their
natural inclinations, which might prevent the
faithful accomplishment of her various duties.
One can easily understand that a child, who endeavoured to eradicate all thoughts of vanity, of self-
complacency, of attachment to the most agreeable
objects, and who was so generous in serving God,
must also have been endowed with similar mastery
over her tongue. That insatiable desire of talking,
which worries some children, originates in their

dislike of the least mortification, and in the unbounded scope they give to all their caprices and
to their most ridiculous desires.

It was not the desire of being esteemed by her
teachers that led Miss Le Ber to conform to silence:
such an interested motive was too vile and too base
for her pure high-minded soul. Her only aim was
the fulfilment of God's divine will, which she rec-
ognized in the rule that ordained silence. She also
hoped by such means to imitate the child Jesus,
who remained silent during his childhood, notwithstanding the consolation he would have found in
conversing with his mother.

The consequence of such holy dispositions was
that Miss Le Ber found silence an easy means of
acquiring interior recollection, and her teachers
add that such was her greatest delight. This recollection was no useless occupation. It united her
more closely to God, it reminded her of His divine
presence, and led her to make frequent interior
acts of love. This opinion is confirmed by the remark her teachers make in the above-mentioned
memoir: "Constant recollection of the Divine
" presence was the result of the profound respect
" she had always manifested towards God's sov-
" ereign majesty."

Such happy dispositions naturally led this holy
child to make great progress in solid virtue. The
thought of God's presence is truly a most efficacious
and infallible means of acquiring all other virtues.
When God chose Abraham for the father of the

faithful, that is, of all perfect souls, He gave him but one commandment: "Walk in my presence and be perfect," as if to let him know that this exercise includes all other virtues; by walking in my presence you will avoid evil, and do good, you will be humble, charitable, patient, finally you will attain the pinnacle of perfection.

Whence comes it, however, that some children seldom endeavour to acquire this holy habit, and always experience such difficulty in thinking of God? The fact is, their hearts are still in the world, are still slaves of all their natural feelings. Such children cannot bear the slightest humiliation, not even the mildest reprimand: their sole motive is the gratification of their various inclinations. They wish to see and hear everything, they seek nought but enjoyment, and never consent to the slightest mortification. They know not what it is to sacrifice to God, an inquisitive look, a useless or uncharitable word, a sensual desire, or an act of self-love. Their eyes and ears are open to see and hear everything, and they are always willing to express their sentiments and desires. This state of habitual thoughtlessness brings with it a distaste for spiritual exercises, rendering it impossible to think of God's presence; and thus exposes youth to innumerable temptations which finally lead them to deplorable errors.

The presence of God became so familiar to Miss Le Ber, that it inspired her with a great love for meditation. She thus greatly edified her teachers, who could not refrain from admiring her. When a soul is fully penetrated with Divine love, she experiences no difficulty in conversing with God; and the more she is detached from created things, the greater will be her ardour to possess the Author of all good; her wishes are then more fully gratified, her contemplation is more enlightened, and her spiritual enjoyment is greatly heightened, for our Lord himself says in the Gospel: " Blessed are the clean of heart, for they shall see God," that is to say, they will not only enjoy His divine presence, but His adorable perfections will be manifested to them in meditation, even during their sojourn in this vale of tears.

This was verified in Miss Le Ber even in her childhood; and it was owing to her endeavours to mortify her senses and all her natural affections, so as to live in continual recollection. Her first teachers confirm this opinion: " Her constant " recollection gave rise to a great taste for medi- " tation, in which her only guide seemed to be the " Divine Spirit. Her zeal for meditation was so " ardent, that when she was but a mere child she " would withdraw from her companions, and was " often found in prayer. When absent from the " recreations taken by all the pupils, she was al- " ways found before the Blessed Sacrament, or in " an oratory in some remote part of the house."

Teachers can be called truly happy, when their efforts are only required to suppress such excesses of fervour. Far from being pernicious to others,

these holy exercises inspire them with feelings of
respect and admiration for the fervent piety which
leads to them ; and teachers can form well-founded
anticipations for their pupils' future welfare. This
was proved by Miss Le Ber.

One may reasonably agree with the Ursulines
in the belief, that this holy child, called by God to
an angelic life, as will be hereafter seen, was induced by the Holy Ghost to separate from her
companions, in order to give indications of her
future destination.

Such instances have been met with in holy individuals, who, in their earliest years, have manifested some striking proof of the extraordinary life
to which they are called. This praiseworthy avi-
dity which induced Miss Le Ber to practise meditation, was also a certain proof of the celestial
consolations this holy exercise afforded her, and
that God was the sole object of her most tender
affections. In return, the Almighty bestowed ineffable consolations on this generous and self-sacrificing soul.

Many children find no delight in meditation or
in any other exercise of piety, because their hearts
are engrossed by unlawful affections, which accompany them everywhere, and which they will not
sacrifice even to God. They consider such exercises as painful and disagreeable ; they accomplish
them unwillingly through routine, and always with
indifference and distaste. If they could only cleanse
their hearts of those affections which sully them,

by performing one perfect act of self sacrifice, the Almighty would reward them most liberally by letting them feel the lightness of His burden, they would then fully appreciate how true it is, that " Blessed are the clean of heart, for they shall see God."

Such children would find greater consolations and more exquisite delight in meditation, and in exercises of piety, than in recreations or in other agreeable pastimes. Finally, they would sigh for the moment when it is given them to return to such exercises ; for experience has proved that therein are found the purest joys, and the most perfect happiness that can be enjoyed here below.

CHAPTER V.

Miss Le Ber's constant recollection of the divine
presence, her desire of communing with God, the
ardour with which she sought all occasions of mental prayer ; her sole aim of pleasing God in all
things, and other holy dispositions, stamped her
existence with an angelic character, and seemed to
associate her with the heavenly spirits, although
she still inhabited a mortal body.

The great veneration she had always manifested
towards the Holy Angels, induced her to select
them for her models. Her teachers inform us:
" that the thought of the Holy Angels who are
" always in God's presence, affected her in a most
" extraordinary manner ; when she reflected on
" those happy spirits, she ever experienced won-
" drous feelings of love and confidence." As this
confidence was founded on the charity of the Holy

Angels and on their power before the Almighty, it led Miss Le Ber to have recourse to them in all her wants; she experienced the efficacy of their intercession in several circumstances, as some subsequent instances of her life will hereafter prove.

Saint Michael and her Guardian Angel were her most ordinary intercessors among the heavenly hierarchy. The archangel Saint Michael inspired her with peculiar confidence, owing to the energy with which he had avenged the Divine honour on the rebel angels, exclaiming: " Who is like unto God ?" This induced her to have frequent recourse to him in temptation, that he might obtain for her that divine strength required in order to triumph in the combats, which we are compelled to wage against the enemy of our salvation. She had still more frequently recourse to her Guardian Angel, as the being to whose care God had committed her at Baptism. It would be no easy task to tell what profound respect and unbounded confidence she always manifested towards the Guardian of her innocence; invoking him in all trying circumstances, often communing interiorly with him; following his inspirations in her doubts. This unalterable fidelity being amply rewarded, tended but to increase her confidence, and to induce her to have more frequent recourse to his intercession.

We cannot doubt that the Holy Angels, being our elder brethren, are united to us by the bonds of true fraternal love, and are very powerful intercessors in our behalf. Each one of us received at

Baptism one of those heavenly spirits to be our
guide through life. Notwithstanding the universality of this belief, how happens it that so few
Christians have recourse to these ever-watchful
guardians, while others are so completely neglect-
ful towards them ? Miss Le Ber's example should
lead us henceforward to honour our Guardian Angel, and to have recourse to him in all our wants,
with a firm conviction, that he can and will assist us.
This holy practice ought to be acquired by young
girls during their stay at school, the better to practise it afterwards during life ; and thus secure these
holy protectors' assistance in all the crosses they
may meet on earth, and particularly at the hour of
death.

A child endowed with such rare spiritual gifts
as our heroine was, could not be deficient in piety
towards the Immaculate Virgin, the fond Mother
of all Christians.   Devotion to Mary was inherent
in Miss Le Ber's nature, and it seems to have been
the foundation of her piety and her subsequent
angelical life.   She gave striking proofs of it when
she became a pupil of the Ursulines.   She considered herself bound to particular devotion to the
Blessed Virgin ; and in a more special manner
than any of her companions, and that on account
of her native city.   She was wont to say, that,
tender and sincere devotion to this Holy Mother
should ever be the peculiar characteristic of all the
inhabitants of Ville Marie, since that city had been
founded, in order to promote the honour of the

Blessed Virgin throughout North America. Although she joined in the honour bestowed on all Mary's mysteries, her natural inclinations led her to prefer those interior dispositions which accompanied the Blessed Virgin's actions, and imparted a high degree of sanctity to even the most insignificant of them. The better to ensure the faithful imitation of Mary's interior life, she united her intentions to the feelings and dispositions which had animated this glorious model during her mortal career. She always thought of this when praying, when working, or when conversing, so that similar actions might be actuated by similar motives. We will not here dwell on her other practices of devotion toward the Blessed Virgin: the remainder of this life will contain an uninterrupted series of means, which she employed to become more and more like unto her Immaculate Mother.

It was by thus uniting her interior dispositions to those of Mary, that she found such delight in honoring Jesus in the adorable Sacrament of the altar. This mystery was always the centre of her devotion, as the continuation of her life will prove. Even in her earliest years, she had exhibited striking proofs of this profound respect. It is also said, that she made her first communion with inexpressible feelings of love and fervour. This can be easily believed, when one is reminded that the Almighty seemed to have poured down his choicest blessings on this favoured child. The fervour she then evinced never afterwards decreased ; which unfortunately is not the case with many young persons. Miss Le Ber endeavoured to increase her fervour, after her departure from the Convent, by her fidelity in preparing herself for the frequent reception of the blessed Eucharist, which was ever the object of her most ardent desires, and to her, the true bread of life.

BOOK SECOND.

CHAPTER I.

MISS LE BER'S FIDELITY IN ATTENDING TO ALL THE EXERCISES OF PIETY WHICH SHE HAD PREVIOUSLY PRACTISED IN THE URSULINE CONVENT.—MODESTY IN HER ATTIRE.

When Miss Le Ber had finished her education, she bade a final adieu to her dear companions, to her beloved teachers, and returned to her family, who still resided at Ville Marie, bearing thither the just sorrow of all who had known her. This happened in 1667, our heroine being then in her fifteenth year. On leaving the convent, she did not alter her way of living, nor did she give up any of her accustomed exercises of piety; for she

well knew that these means of sanctification would
be more necessary now, on account of the many
dangers to which she would be exposed. This
knowledge of the world even led her to add new
devotions, to those she had long since adopted;
thus differing greatly from those young persons,
who, not having cultivated a true spirit of piety
during their stay in religious communities, rejoice
at the prospect of being free from such exercises
in the paternal mansion. But, unfortunately, they
make a bad use of this fatal liberty, by abandoning
their devotions, when they most require them, by
laying down the strong arms of prayer, when the
moment of combat is nigh.

But Miss Le Ber, this truly wise and prudent
virgin, acted very differently. As soon as she returned home, her first care, with her director's
approbation, was to draw up a rule of life wherein
she divided her time with great discernment,
alloting different portions to prayer, reading,
embroidery, and other domestic duties. Her
pious parents, being convinced that to second her
fervent dispositions, would be the greatest proof of
affection, afforded her every possible means of ac-
quitting herself of her religious practices; and even
took pleasure in noticing her fidelity, although
some of these practices appeared rather extraordinary in a young girl of fifteen.

She rose every morning very early, and, before
her manual occupations, devoted an entire hour to
mental prayer, previous to assisting at the first

D

parochial mass, which she attended regularly. Her lively and ardent faith in the dogma of the real presence of our Lord in the Holy Eucharist, inspired her with the practice of prostrating herself, and of kissing the ground, at the elevation of the Sacred Host. This action she always performed with most profound religious feelings, and with such sincere humility that she edified all who saw her. She acted in like manner before approaching the Holy Table, when about to enjoy the happiness of communicating with our dear Lord in His sacrament of Love, which happened very frequently. Although this practice of kissing the ground may now appear rather singular, at that time it edified all the faithful, owing to the simplicity and fervour then reigning throughout the colony. When Miss Le Ber received Holy Communion, she was wont to withdraw to the most retired part of the church, the better to avoid all distractions and public notice, and to give vent to transports of holy joy during her thanksgiving, which she endeavoured to lengthen as much as possible.

The inclemency of the weather never prevented her from paying a daily visit to the Blessed Sacrament, thus rendering homage to Jesus Christ, really present on the altar. While there, she impressed all present with a profound feeling of respect, in beholding the touching modesty, and seraphic fervour, with which she expressed her feelings of adoration, love, and confidence towards her Beloved.

We may here remark, that the year after Miss Le Ber had left the convent, her father and her uncle, Mr. Lemoyne, desiring to give a public testimony of their profound respect for Jesus Christ, concealed under the sacramental veils, presented a silver lamp to the parochial church, that it might burn night and day before the tabernacle. But the daily homage offered by Mr. Le Ber's daughter, that terrestrial angel, was a still more striking testimonial of religious feeling, both before God and before men.

Miss Le Ber edified the whole parish by her modesty and by her fervent piety, not only when she assisted at the Holy Sacrifice of the Mass, when she received Holy Communion, and when she visited the Blessed Sacrament, but also while practising less important acts of religion; for instance, when she presented the blessed bread at High Mass, and what is still more remarkable, even when she collected in the church on Sunday, which she always did in her turn. This custom then existed at Ville Marie; but it has since been abolished, owing to the abuses to which it gave rise, when fervour had decreased. .

Finally, Miss Le Ber's modest deportment in the streets greatly edified all the citizens. Whether going to Church, or returning from it, she was never seen to stop on the way to converse with her acquaintances, nor to enter any house to visit its inmates; for she found time too precious, to be thus idly squandered. Apart from the conversations she had with her parents, and those she sometimes held with the Hospital Nuns, and the Sisters of the Congregation of Notre Dame, as we shall soon see, her time was wholly devoted to spiritual lectures, work, and prayer.

Miss Le Ber's dislike of the world did not originate in a fear of occupying a disadvantageous position in it; for she might have held a very distinguished rank, and been much sought for. Among the Canadian young ladies she was undoubtedly the one in whom was centered all that the world so highly honours. She was not void of grace and beauty; and those exterior advantages were heightened by natural wit and penetration, improved by careful education, which adorned her mind with useful and agreeable knowledge. Her naturally good and generous disposition was enhanced by her modesty, her unaffected gaiety, and her sweet gravity. Such qualities gave her great ascendancy over all those who surrounded her. Polite, affable, and always willing to conform to adopted customs, she acted so easily and gracefully that she pleased all around her. Belonging to the richest family in the country at that time, and, as an only daughter, being a special favourite of her parents, they determined upon giving her a dower of fifty thousand *écus** : thus rendering her the richest heiress in New France.

As her parents intended that she should hold a

---

* An old French coin, worth about 55 cents of American money.

distinguished position in the world after she had left
the Convent, they desired her to dress in such a
manner as to suit their views, which were quite conformable to her condition of life.   Although Miss
Le Ber had always experienced a great distaste for
worldly ornaments, she submitted her will to her
parents, and accepted, through obedience, whatever
apparel they destined for her.   It is true that the
purely religious feelings which actuated both Mr.
and Mrs. Le Ber, and their delicate and enlightened conscience, prevented them from adopting any
style of dress condemned by Christian modesty; for
they well knew, that, owing to the variety of con-
ditions which has existed since man's disobedience,
God has allowed persons of higher ranks to be distinguished from others, in their style of dress, as
trees are known by the variety of their fruit and
foliage; but this distinction must never trespass on
the limits of modesty, which should be equally sacred
and equally respected in all ranks of society.   They
were also aware that persons occupying an elevated
position, are more strictly bound to conform most
scrupulously to this principle, on account of the
influence of their example, which the lower classes
endeavor to follow, not only in the form of wearing-
apparel, but also in the liberty of dress.

But, alas! how many evils have followed from
a neglect of this important duty.   How many immodest fashions have been introduced into entire
Parishes, by the vanity of some mothers who allowed their children to adopt them; and these

persons, occupying distinguished positions, have been imitated by others. Numberless sins have unfortunately been caused by immodesty, which, from being but partially concealed, becomes the more pernicious and the more criminal in its consequences. This false veil is merely an additional means of corruption, used to induce a young person to set aside all restraint, and to lead others to banish all delicacy. Thus, by a subversion in the order of things, those whom God raised to distinguished social positions, so that they may lead others to Him by word and example, seem to combine their united efforts to lose souls, by banishing from their hearts all thoughts of virtue and innocence.

Although Miss Le Ber's obedience to her pious parents, had led her to accept costly apparel, which was however always regulated by modesty; her consummate virtue never allowed her to find therein, thoughts of vanity, or even the smallest degree of self-complacency. The horror with which she had always viewed the pomps of the world, inspired her also with distaste for fastidiousness in her style of dress; those brilliant outfits, which are generally, for other young persons, a source of ostentation, and of a desire of winning admiration, afforded her so many opportunities of performing meritorious and virtuous actions.

As Esther of old, our admirable heroine, when obliged to wear superfluous ornaments, would humble herself before God, with many interior protestations of fidelity to Him alone. The better to nurture these Christian sentiments in her heart, she always, notwithstanding the delicacy of her constitution, wore instruments of penance concealed beneath her costly garments.

Young persons who take similar precautions, when obliged to indulge in some ornamental style of dress, need fear, neither for themselves, nor for others, notwithstanding the costliness of their apparel; provided that, like Miss Le Ber's, it be always suitable and modest.

CHAPTER II.

THE BETTER TO PRESERVE HER INNOCENCE,
MISS LE BER AVOIDS WORLDLY ASSEMBLIES.
PAYS FREQUENT VISITS TO THE SISTERS
OF THE CONGREGATION DE NOTRE DAME.

Although Miss Le Ber's parents intended her for
a married life, and desired that she should dress
according to her rank; yet they never brought her
forward in those brilliant assemblies which take
place in the world; nor even in more limited social
circles, composed but of a small number of friends
and acquaintances; convinced that the latter are
often as dangerous as the former. They were too sincerely attached to their daughter, to expose her to
lose her innocence : a treasure, incomparably greater
than any they could bestow; since it alone, could
render her truly happy. Their conduct, in this
respect, may appear too severe, to many so called
Christian parents ; but, alas ! many are strangely
deluded on these important matters.

Their daughters have scarcely left school, when
they are ushered into private assemblies. They say

that their intention, in doing so, is to form their manners, and to give them a knowledge of the world. They do not reflect, that, by thus exposing them to many dangers, they initiate them into vice, hitherto unknown. They forget, that, at this critical age, a young person has to combat sufficient interior enemies who are incessantly attacking her imagination and heart. Besides, these private assemblies give rise to many evils, without exposing her in such reunions to a multitude of others more perfidious and more dangerous. The choice of the guests, the confidence evinced, and freedom allowed to friends and acquaintances, the conversations which are held, the amusements which take place; finally, all tends to produce the most fatal impressions, on a young girl who is aware that every eye is fixed upon her, and that she is become an object of special attention. This conduct, which exposes her to so many dangers, is a conspiracy against innocence, or, to say the least, an open provocation of God's goodness; particularly, when the approving looks of a father and mother lead her to believe that such amusements are legitimate. If such parents are still Christians, how can they hope that a young girl's heart, which is naturally so weak and inclined to form attachments, can remain faithful to God in the midst of such innumerable enticements ? Angelical virtue could scarcely undergo this ordeal.

Mr. and Mrs. Le Ber being fully instructed in the manner of fulfilling this important duty, and being most sincerely attached to their daughter, used every means in their power to keep her heart pure and unsullied. Though kind and affable towards all, she never centered her affections in particular on any one. The only persons whom she visited were the Hospital Nuns, and the Sisters of the rising institution of the Congregation de Notre Dame; not that she desired to enter either of these Institutions, for the monastic life had no attractions for her; but merely to talk of God with the kind religious, and to stimulate herself to the practice of virtue by their holy conversation.

Among the nuns of St. Joseph, she most frequently visited Mother Macé, whom the entire community venerated as a living relic. Our heroine had become acquainted with this religious when a child, during her visits to Mlle. Mance, at the Hôtel-Dieu. On her return from school, she renewed the acquaintance, and continued to visit her very frequently, until the moment of her reclusion, of which we shall soon speak. But her most confidential friend was sister Margaret Bourgeoys, who had been destined by the Almighty to sanctify the young persons of this rising colony, and who was then founding the institution since known, as the Congrégation de Notre Dame. The favorable impressions produced on Miss Le Ber by conversing with this holy foundress, the atmosphere of sanctity which seemed to pervade the Congregation, the tender piety there manifested towards the Blessed Virgin Mary, who was honored as Superioress, as Queen and Mother of this Institute, its appellation, *Congrégation de Notre Dame :*—these and many other motives gave rise to Miss Le Ber's well-founded predilection ; as also to a profound veneration and to an unchangeable attachment to this holy house, of which she became one of the most illustrious benefactresses. Miss Le Ber was so devoted to the Blessed Virgin, and so desirous of procuring Her honor that her acquaintance with Sister Bourgeoys soon ripened into a friendship, which was daily strenghtened by their mutual devotion to the Mother of God; for the Foundress of the Congregation had willingly severed all ties of Home and kindred in the hope that, by so doing, she might lead the youthful generation of this rising colony to love and honor Mary. This thought had borne her up in all her trials, and had induced her to submit voluntarily to all the privations, which had fallen to her lot since her first departure from her native country. A fact worthy of note is, that the chapel in honor of Notre Dame de Bonsecours was erected in 1678 by the zealous efforts of Sister Bourgeoys, a year after Miss Le Ber had left school. The motive which led to the erection of this chapel was a desire of increasing devotion towards Mary. This opinion is confirmed by a public act registered by Sister Bourgeoys at the Prothonotary's office, on the 24th of June of the same year. "As the Sisters of the Congrégation de " Notre Dame," says she in this memorable act, " wish that the devotion which they have always " had for the Blessed Virgin, their Mother, their

" Foundress, and the Protectress of their order,
" would daily increase, and become more general
" in Montreal than it has been until this date ; that
" it might likewise be transmitted to posterity ;
" they requested and obtained that the chapel,
" which they had erected, might be annexed to the
" parish, and serve for public devotion ; that the
" Blessed Virgin might be honored therein, under
" the title of Notre Dame de Bonsecours." This
prophetic declaration made by Sister Bourgeoys, is
literally fulfilled, even at the present day, by the
spontaneous concourse of innumerable pilgrims
who resort thither, and who are quite ignorant that
it ever was made. This declaration, inspired by
God alone, would be sufficient to prove Sister
Bourgeoys' divine mission in the colony : and is
also a proof of Miss Le Ber's discernment and
sound wisdom in choosing this estimable person
to be her confidential friend.

In 1672, Sister Bourgeoys brought out with her
from France twelve or thirteen assistants, who were
all partakers of her zeal and fervor. She was also
surrounded by a certain number of young persons
born at Ville Marie, whom she had trained from
childhood, and who were about to fulfil various offices in the community of the Congrégation de
Notre Dame. Several among them were related to
Miss Le Ber, particularly two, Frances and Margaret Lemoyne, who were her cousins. The entire detachment from all earthly things practised
by these Christian virgins, their sincere humility,
their evangelical simplicity, their love of poverty,

their zeal and generosity for the sanctification of
souls; in a word, the practice of all those virtues
which so greatly edified the colonists, were for Miss
Le Ber, a sort of celestial perfume which led her
frequently to the Congrégation de Notre Dame,
where her visits were also a source of great satisfaction to the sisterhood, from the fact that she herself was a subject of peculiar edification.

Our heroine considered all these young persons
as so many models of fervour; but, by a special
permission from on high, one of them gained still
stronger ascendancy over her youthful affections.
She was one of those privileged souls who, from
the abundant graces she received, and from her
fidelity in corresponding to them, seemed to ad-
vance with astonishing rapidity in the ways of
that entire detachment which Miss Le Ber was so
desirous of acquiring. As their conversations
always tended to unite our heroine more
closely to God, the attachment became greater.
Solid virtue alone was the foundation of this
friendship. God destined it as a means of leading
Miss Le Ber to still greater perfection, and more
absolute detachment from the world and all earthly
things. She never left this holy friend without
feeling a singular attraction towards universal
detachment. God, to give her an opportunity
of practising this abnegation so necessary to a perfect life, was pleased to deprive her of the presence
and advice of this holy friend; whom He called to
Himself, shortly afterwards.

CHAPTER III.

THE EDIFYING DEATH OF ONE OF THE SISTERS
OF THE CONGRÉGATION DE NOTRE DAME,
INDUCES MISS LE BER TO LIVE ENTIRELY
APART FROM THE WORLD.—SHE MAKES A
VOW OF CHASTITY FOR FIVE YEARS.

The holy friend of whom we have spoken was a
fruit ripe for heaven; for, notwithstanding her
youth, she had already reached the pinnacle of
perfection. It seemed as if Miss Le Ber's friendship had been allowed, the better to enable her to
make an agreeable sacrifice to God, which drew
down upon her most abundant blessings. As human
friendships are founded upon natural motives, they
separate hearts from God, by attaching them one to
another; but sacred ties tend, on the contrary, to
unite all affections more closely to the Creator;
their first beginning, and last end. So death, far
from sundering such ties, purifies them and renders
them still more lasting; for it excites a desire of
imitating the lost friends, so as to be sharers in
the happiness they enjoy before the throne of

God : but when purely human bonds are formed between those whose hopes do not extend beyond the grave, then is the separation truly painful, for it leaves nought but bitterness, affliction, and despair.

The death of a young Corinthian maiden was bitterly felt by a faithful attendant who was most tenderly attached to her. As a means of alleviating her grief, she collected various articles which the young girl had valued during her lifetime, and placed them in a wicker basket on her tomb ; covering them carefully with a tile, so that the rain might not injure them.*   This vain homage was the sole tribute that a pagan could offer to her, whose loss she mourned ; it was her only token of affection, as it was also her only means of lessening the heart-

---

* Vitruvius, who relates this trait, adds : It happened that a root of Acanthus lay on the spot where the basket was placed. When spring came, the plant grew, and spread among the openings around the basket; thus the leaves and branches protruded wherever an aperture was found ; their various folds giving the whole a very graceful appearance. The sculptor Callimachus, surnamed the *Industrious*, by the Athenians, was struck with the elegant appearance which the leaves gave the basket. He thought that an ornament of the same shape would form an elegant summit for the columns then used in constructing edifices. Architecture is indebted to this able artist, for the elegance and grandeur which characterize Corinthian capitals. Such was the origin of these capitals, called Corinthian because first used in Corinth.

rending sorrow caused by that death which filled her soul with bitterness. The Incarnation of the Son of God not having yet reunited those ties sundered by man's disobedience, this was indeed the only consolation pagans could enjoy, when death parted them from those who were near and dear to them : as Saint Paul says, they beheld death with fear and trembling, and no hope lessened their affliction.

But the impressions made on Miss Le Ber by her holy friend's death, differed much from pagan despair : all she beheld was replete with hope and consolation. This worthy follower of Sister Bourgeoys had given such edifying examples of piety, of obedience, and of patience, during all her sufferings ; she had evinced such inexpressible joy at the thought of quitting the world to be inseparably united to God ; she seemed so anxious for that hour of her indissoluble union with her Divine spouse, her soul being filled with such unspeakable delight and happiness while she peacefully breathed her last ; all this made such a profound impression on Miss Le Ber, that, from that moment, she considered she had done nothing for God, and resolved to consecrate herself entirely to Him. These resolutions were strengthened on beholding the remains of her holy friend : death seemed to add new charms to that now inanimate form. The perfect calmness and celestial expression of mildness, innocence, and sanctity, which beautified her countenance, aroused within Miss Le Ber's heart, feelings of holy emulation to walk in the footsteps of her departed friend. Her sole ambition from that day, was to become more thoroughly penetrated with all her friend's dispositions, that she might one day merit the grace of so happy a death.

Judging from the effects which this event produced, one might be led to suppose that the deceased had assumed a new life in the person of Miss Le Ber, and that, in the separation of body and soul, her spirit of entire consecration to God and of absolute detachment from the world had been communicated to our heroine. It was immediately after this edifying death, that Miss Le Ber took the generous, but astonishing resolution which she soon after executed. As the religious life did not possess any attraction for her, she intended to live in her own home, with as much recollection and separation from the world, as could be practised in the most fervent communities, and to imitate those saints whom she most admired on account of their union with God.

Such was the state of her mind, when a proposal of marriage induced her to carry out her design without further delay, and inspired her with a still greater distaste for the world, than she had hitherto experienced. As her parents had always intended that she should remain in the world, they were very desirous that she should contract this alliance, which was most honorable and conformable to their desires. They neglected nothing to obtain her consent; but all their efforts proved

E

abortive, or rather tended but to increase her opposition to such a union. The more they expatiated on the advantages and enjoyments which might be hers in the world, the more she despised them. Her parents, edified by the virtue of their worthy daughter, ceased to urge her any longer. They consented that she should lead a single life in her own home, there live in entire solitude, not imagining to what a degree she would carry her love of silence and retreat.

So far, Miss Le Ber's life has presented nothing which could prevent its being offered to the imitation of all young persons desirous of sanctifying themselves in the world. Faithful in the paternal mansion to all the exercises of piety she had practised in the convent: the better to conform to her parents desires, she avoided any style of dress that would have distinguished her from others. She refrained from appearing in worldly assemblies and in meetings where her virtue would be exposed; her only connections were persons whose holy examples were calculated to edify her. All Christian virgins who wish to be faithful to their baptismal vows are so far bound to imitate her. If Miss Le Ber's life from this date, cannot serve as a model for young persons in the world, her example will, at least, lead them to renewed fervour in the fulfilment of their various duties, by proving the power of grace over souls. To accomplish the generous resolution which she had taken after her friend's death, of living in entire seclusion from the world, she desired to unite herself more closely to God, by a vow of perpetual chastity. The naturally virtuous inclinations which she had evinced from her earliest years, her invincible dislike to all earthly grandeur, her refusal of the offer which she had received, the strong impressions of grace produced by her holy friend's death, and the innocent life which she had always led;—all these motives seemed sufficient to procure for her the happiness of making this vow.

Notwithstanding all these reasons, Mr. Séguenot, priest of the Seminary of Saint Sulpice, who had first guided her steps in the path of virtue; thought proper that she should not then contract any perpetual obligation. Although he had no reason to doubt the solidity of her resolutions, or her constancy in fulfilling them, he found her too young to bind herself irrevocably by vows.

This occurred in 1679, Miss Le Ber being in her seventeenth year. He advised her to take the vow for five years; so that, after this trial, she might be free to act according to her inclinations: and if she still persevered in her resolution to have no other spouse but Jesus Christ, she might then bind herself by a perpetual vow. Notwithstanding her great desire of contracting an irrevocable engagement, she willingly submitted to her confessor's decision; for never before, perhaps, had any one beheld such profound and entire obedience as that which our heroine practised to all persons whom God had placed over her. Although she was obliged to limit the duration of her vow, the obligation nowise lessened the fervour with which she pronounced it. This can be easily understood when one reflects that this pure soul was already far advanced in perfection, and sighed for God alone.

This vow, although it did not alter her manner of living, enforced what she had hitherto most willingly practised; and tended to increase her fervour, and to strengthen the celestial flame of divine love which already burned within her. The thought that she was Jesus' favoured spouse, induced her to consecrate herself wholly to Him, by offering Him her heart, her thoughts, and all her affections. She applied to herself those words of the Canticle of Canticles, addressed by the heavenly spouse to the faithful soul, to excite her to a perfect fidelity and delicacy of love;" my sister, my beloved, place me as a seal on thy heart and on thy arm." Hence, she desired that her heart should be closed and sealed to all that was not Jesus; that all thoughts which did not emanate from Jesus should be banished; finally, she desired that he should be as a seal on her arm—that is to say, that all her actions (figured in Scripture by hands and arms) should have no other end but the glory of Jesus,—no other motive but his pure love. The better to realise this, she after long and repeated solicitations, obtained permission to give up all intercourse with the world, and to lead a most retired life in her own house, as the following chapter will relate.

CHAPTER IV.

MISS LE BER IS CALLED TO LIVE IN SECLUSION IN HER FATHER'S HOUSE. HER PIOUS PARENTS ACCEDE TO HER DESIRE.

The Holy Ghost, sole sanctifier of the Church, arouses within the hearts of the faithful a desire of avoiding sin and detachment from creatures to be more closely united to God alone. For this purpose, this Divine Spirit raised up, in preceding ages, men of eminent virtue in whom this horror of sin and detachment from the world was manifested in a very high degree. The celebrated solitaries and world-renowned anchorites, St. Paul the Hermit, St. Anthony, and many others, who peopled the ancient deserts, and whose life seemed to be one continued miracle ; what were they, but powerful preachers, whose flight from the world and holiness of life openly condemned the pagans' sensual and profane manner of living, while they stimulated the faithful to the exact fulfilment of all these duties. This sort of silent preaching has always been most efficacious. Among other in-

stances, history presents us with the numerous con-
versions which took place among the crowds who
flocked around the pillar of Saint Simeon Stylite
to behold the holy hermit.

To produce similar effects among the weaker sex,
God allowed, that, from the first ages of Christianity, there should not only be far-famed penitents,
such as a Saint Mary of Egypt, but that spotless
virgins should isolate themselves entirely from the
world, and live in perpetual voluntary reclusion,
holding communication with no other, save those
chosen to attend their indispensable wants. Sulpicius Severus remarks in his dialogues, that these
examples were very frequent during Saint Martin's
time.* The fervour evinced by these virgins who
lived without any intercourse with the exterior
world, appears to have given rise to cloistered communities subsequently formed on the same plan;
this was also allowed by Divine Providence as a
means of strengthening faith in those persons who
had but lately embraced Christianity, and to
induce them to aspire to perfection.

God wished to renew this prodigy in the Catholic
Church in Canada: hence, Miss Le Ber was
chosen as an unparalleled example for all young
persons in America, and one well suited to excite
their fervour. Thus it was that the same Divine

(*) *Sulpicii Severi, Dialog.* II, *de Virtutib. Martini,*
B. Martinus magnificans Virginis illius reclusæ, cum
exultatione virtutem, *inusitato, in his duntaxat regioni-
bus,* gaudebat *exemplo.*

Spirit who had inspired the first recluses with their generous and heroic determination of entire separation from the world, also led Miss Le Ber to choose a similar line of conduct; and our heroine was not less favoured than those admirable virgins who had received from above the strength and constancy requisite to follow it until their last breath.

She was at first led to imitate the reclusion of Saint Catherine of Sienna, who had remained some time in a cell in her father's house so as to live more closely united to God. When Miss Le Ber first intimated her design to her parents, they were naturally both surprised and afflicted, for she wished to break all intercouse, not only with strangers but even with themselves, and that in their declining years. Notwithstanding their piety, such a resolution taken by their only daughter, the sole object of their most tender affections, must have been a severe blow particularly as this cherished child's superior qualities had made them consider her as the legitimate source of all their joy and consolation.

Judging from Miss Le Ber's love of retreat, one must not believe that hers was one of those dull and melancholy characters; ill suited for society, and void of all attraction and amiability. Far from being sullen and morose, she was remarkable for a quick and penetrating mind, for mild and agreeable manners, and for a most interesting conversation; replete with vivacity and ingenuity, when the subject suited her taste ; that is, when it related to piety ; because one of her invariable rules was never to converse on any other topic. One can easily perceive, that, with such qualities, having had all that was necessary to render her the delight of her parents, so pious and virtuous themselves ; such a design of giving up all intercouse with them, however pure the motives, could not but afflict them.

Hence, they deferred acquiescing to her desire, and that prudence, which is inseparable from true Christian piety, guided their conduct. But after mature deliberation on the nature and consequences of such a step, after consulting the most disinterested and enlightened persons, they finally agreed to offer this sacrifice to God ; for they acknowledged that the Almighty had inspired their daughter with this design, and that the fulfilment of it was destined for His Glory and the sanctification of souls. Subsequent events proved the truth of this opinion.

While reading this life, many may be astonished that Mr. and Mrs. Le Ber consented to their daughter's reclusion : they may even think that the motive which led them to do so, was a ridiculous devotion, which differed vastly from a truly religious spirit. A few remarks on this important matter may not only contribute to explain, to see and to justify Mr. Le Ber, but also to remove illusions in which so many are prone to indulge.

Parents are intended by God as representatives

of His paternal solicitude ; and that love which children bear them should have God alone in view.
Hence, when truly Christian children give their
parents any proof of affection, it is not merely
through a desire of satisfying their natural inclination.   A propensity which is common to brutes, is
far too terrestrial and too base for a Christian soul·
These proofs of affection should be given to God,
whom they reverence in their parents ; and this view
of God, far from weakening filial love, tends to
strengthen and elevate it, and renders it constant and
unchangeable.   A child actuated merely by natural
motives, is all affection for his parents, while he
receives from them, reciprocal marks of tenderness;
but he who honors God in the person of his parents,
will always love them notwithstanding their faults,
as fondly as if they were the most accomplished
persons in the world.   His fondness continues unchangeable in the midst of persecution, and unjust
treatment meets with the same return, as kindness
and benevolence.   This is owing to the fact that
God is equally deserving of respect and honor, under whatever envelope he may hide his authority.

God had thought proper to enlighten the French
colonists in Canada, by inspiring them all, with a
special devotion towards Jesus, Mary, and Joseph,
that Holy Family, the model of all Christian families.   Children were thus taught how to fulfil
their duties towards their parents, and they in
turn learned how pure should be the love which
they owed their offspring.   Each individual en-

deavoured to mould his conduct on that of this
sublime original : children took the child Jesus
for their model, while fathers sought to imitate
Saint Joseph, and mothers neglected no means
to resemble the Blessed Virgin.* The child
Jesus loved both Mary and Saint Joseph, through
love for God, and because they were His representatives. Notwithstanding their manifold perfec-

---

(*) Mention is made in Miss Mance's life of the institution of the confraternity of the Holy Family, and of
its rapid extension throughout Canada. A most striking testimony of the first colonists' zeal, is still found
at the prothonotary's office in Montreal. On the 27th of
January 1663, one hundred and forty citizens of Ville
Marie, accepting Mr. de Maisonneuve's invitation, came
forward of their own accord to form the militia of the
Holy Family ; they were divided into detachments each
containing 7 men, twenty detachments thus forming the
total 140, such was the number of men then capable
of bearing arms at Ville Marie. Mr. Jacques Le Ber's
name is in the eighth detachment, with that of his
brother-in-law, Mr. Charles Lemoyne, of Longueuil.
Mr. de Maisonneuve thus explains his design, in the
preface of this catalogue. " Having been informed
" that the Iroquois intend to attack this place, we call-
" ed to mind that this Island was specially consecrated
" to the Blessed Virgin ; and therefore considered it our
" bounden duty to exhort all her faithful servants to
" unite in defending her dominion. We hereby order
" that the following names be registered at the protho-
" notary's office as an honorable testimonial in favour
" of the bearers, who have thus consented to expose
" their life to defend our Lady's interest and the public
" weal."

tions and the benefits which they conferred upon
Him, He loved them not for themselves alone, but
because His Heavenly Father had sent them to
watch over Him.   When He gave them any proofs
of affection, He revered them for the Eternal
Father.   Such was the model which Miss Le Ber
endeavoured to imitate in her affection for her parents. She loved them for God alone ; and the marks
of respect and fondness which she gave them, might
be considered as so many acts of religion; for God
alone was their object.   She well knew that God,
the Father of all, has the strongest claims on our
obedience ; and when thoroughly convinced that
the Almighty desired her withdrawal from the world
and even from all intercourse with her parents; she
wavered not as to which path she should follow.
In acting thus, she imitated the child Jesus who
parted with Mary and Joseph, heedless both of
their tears, and of the love He bore them; because
His Heavenly Father exacted this separation. She
was also aware, that as Jesus had first taught fidelity to God's will by His example, He had subsequently confirmed it by these words: He who
gives up father and mother, brother and sister to
work for God's kingdom, that is for the Church,
will receive a hundred fold in this world, and eternal happiness in the world to come.

On the other hand, although Miss Le Ber's pious
parents were most tenderly attached to her; they
loved her not for her own sake; they did not even
love her because she was amiable, virtuous, and

accomplished; their fondness sprung from a nobler source; they loved her because they considered her as a being created to God's likeness and as the chosen temple of the Most High : God was the centre of the love which they lavished upon her; they thus differed vastly from those parents, who, losing all sight of God, fairly idolize their children, and who from the pernicious habit of never attributing to God the affection shown them by their children, centre it all in themselves, as if they were mere idols.   Both Mr. and Mrs. Le Ber acted very differently, and always attributed to God all the proofs of affection given them by their daughter; they thus endeavoured to imitate Mary and Joseph, whom they had chosen for their models.   When Mary and Joseph bestowed any marks of tenderness on the child Jesus, they sought not to satisfy any natural propensity; their sole aim was to testify their love towards the Word made flesh : and their caresses were not intended for Jesus' Humanity but for his Divinity.

In like manner do we, in adoring the blessed Eucharist, render homage not to our Saviour's corporeal presence solely, but to the Divinity to which it is united.   The primitive Christians, animated by the same spirit which guided the Holy Family, thus loved their children.   Among many examples, we select the following.   The holy martyr Saint Leonidas was wont to uncover the bosom of his son Origen, when he was a child, and kiss it most respectfully as the temple of the Holy Ghost.

When God's will was expressly made known to Mr. and Mrs. Le Ber, they no longer opposed it, though it required many personal sacrifices. They knew that Mary and Joseph, whom they had chosen for their models, would never have urged the child Jesus to remain with them, when His Heavenly Father had ordained otherwise ; and far from considering the great privation which a separation would impose upon them, they would have done their utmost to direct the Holy Child in the path wherein the Almighty Father desired that He should walk.

As such maxims of true Christian piety had always been impressed on Miss Le Ber's mind, we cannot be surprised at the heroism with which she overcame all natural sensibility, and the firmness and constancy with which she first requested her parents to accede to her desire. The Holy Ghost always fills the heart of Christian children, with that zeal and magnanimity requisite to induce parents to fulfil their duties conscientiously. When Origen, of whom we have just spoken, heard that his father Leonidas had been imprisoned by the persecutors of Christianity ; this pious child, endeavoured by all possible means to visit his father, in order to exhort him to endure martyrdom rather than renounce his Faith. His mother seeing that threats and caresses proved alike incapable of deterring him, and finding no means of retaining him ; concealed his clothes, so as to exclude all possibility of quitting his dwelling. His design having been thus frustrated, he wrote a most ardent letter to his father; from which we shall cite a remarkable passage : " Be firm and do not allow any thought of us to trouble you ;" this was to remove all anxiety from Leonidas who was separated from six sons, all younger than Origen.

We have selected this trait to illustrate the generous sacrifice thus offered to God, both by Miss Le Ber, and by her worthy parents; and to prove a striking resemblance between the primitive Church, and the first years of Catholicity in Canada. If such heroic virtue excite not our admiration, it must be, that fervour has greatly decreased; and that the religious feelings which animated the first colonists are almost extinct among us.

CHAPTER V.

When Mr. Séguenot and other priests of the Seminary, consulted on Miss Le Ber's calling, had seriously reflected, they agreed in considering her inclination for solitude as a divine inspiration, and concluded that if such an extraordinary life were embraced by a young person such as Miss Le Ber, her example would greatly contribute to God's glory, and to the edification of the faithful. They also concurred in the opinion, that, instead of pronouncing any final vow, as she had hoped to do; the wisest plan for her, was to try for awhile, this manner of living. Five years was the time appointed for the Novitiate, which was to begin in 1680. They also added that Miss Le Ber's director, would be at liberty to restrict or relax his penitent's rule of life, according to the exigencies of unforeseen circumstances.

As soon as, this long-wished-for permission was granted, she deferred not a single day, but immediately took up her abode, in the unpretending apartment, which was henceforth, destined to be the sole witness of her angelic fervour. Her father's house opened on Saint Paul street, and was situated very near the Church adjoining the Hôtel-Dieu, then considered the Parish Church; the side of his residence, in the rear of this Church, was the secluded part of the house, that Miss Le Ber chose for her retreat; there, she wished to dwell without entertaining the slightest communication with any one; save, the person appointed to minister to her wants, and to whom a special permission of entering her apartment, when absolutely necessary, had been granted. Scarcely had she entered this voluntary solitude, than considering herself a victim chosen to expiate both her own offences, and those of her fellow-citizens, she immediately adopted an under-garment of hair-cloth, to which she sometimes added a belt of similar material; these instruments of penance were set aside, but to be replaced by others more painful. She even went so far as to macerate her body in the most cruel manner. Were we not aware that the purest souls are those, who, through a spirit of penance, practise the greatest mortifications; the austerities of which we have just spoken, would be a source of amazement, particularly when we reflect not only on the delicate constitution of her who practised them, but also on the holy life which she had previously led. Spotless purity is in itself a great incentive to mortification, by constituting a striking resemblance between pure souls and Jesus Christ; rendering them more worthy to be offered in union with the Immaculate Lamb to expiate the crimes of man.

In embracing this manner of living, Miss Le Ber had given up all communication with the world and was no longer bound down to its exigencies; she resolved therefore to wear linen of the coarsest texture, inferior to that, then, worn by the poorest classes; her outer garments were made of woollen material, and of a very simple form. The same simplicity and poverty were observed in her diet. When some choice or delicate food was offered her, she accepted it, to conceal her mortification, but it generally remained untasted. She even requested her attendant to bring her secretly, the bread which was left after the servants' meals. This request was very unwillingly complied with; but as it seemed to be a source of pleasure to our admirable heroine, these fragments of bread were brought to her, and became her ordinary food. She took so small a quantity of victuals, and of this bread, which was sometimes, most unpalatable, that many could not understand how life could be prolonged, by so little food.

In language and taste she was equally mortified; the better to practise silence during her simple repasts, she ate only when the servant had left her cell. Her entire obedience to her spiritual director

F

was the only preventive from carrying her mortifications still further.

On entering her cell, Miss Le Ber had given up
all communication with her parents, and would
willingly have embraced perpetual reclusion, had
she not been obliged to go daily, to the Parish
Church to attend her religious duties. She arose
every morning at half past four. The inclemency
of the weather never prevented her from attending
the five o'clock mass, both in winter and summer.
On these occasions she was followed by her attendant who was always struck by her extreme modesty. On Sundays and holy days she attended both
mass and vespers.

Her time was distributed in the following manner. She devoted an hour every morning to mental prayer, and then recited a part of the Little Office
of the Blessed Virgin. At eleven o'clock, examination of conscience, as she had seen practised by the
Sisters of the Congregation de Notre Dame. In the
afternoon she employed half an hour in spiritual
reading; after which, she recited the remainder of
the Office and the whole of the Rosary. After her
very frugal evening repast, another half-hour was
devoted to mental prayer. Finally, when the darkness of night had enveloped all in slumber, our
angelic heroine would rise from her hard bed, and
even in the depth of winter, would move towards
the spot where the Blessed Sacrament resided.
There, she would spend a whole hour in adoration
before her heavenly spouse; the light which

burned before the tabernacle being but a feeble image of the ardour of her pure soul. Her sweetest hours were those of this silent midnight adoration of Jesus Christ, in the most holy Sacrament. She used to say that she offered it as a slight atonement, for the worship refused him, by most Christians, then wrapped in slumber.

Such was her life during the five years of trial, and which, she continued as long as she remained a recluse in her father's house; that is, from 1680 until 1695, when she took up her abode in the Congregation de Notre Dame, as shall be mentioned after relating some facts, worthy of notice which occurred during her seclusion beneath the paternal roof.

Miss Le Ber's entire separation from the world, from all social intercourse, and even from all communication with her parents, is a proof, that, in forming the church in Canada, the Almighty had chosen this admirable child of grace to renew in this infant colony, that spirit which had animated so many female recluses, during the primitive ages of the church. We shall here mention a very memorable instance, which elicited the admiration of antiquity, and even that of the Thaumaturgus of the Gauls, the illustrious St. Martin of Tours. It may edify our readers, and prevent any erroneous ideas, which might hereafter arise from Miss Le Ber's great fidelity to reclusion.

Sulpicius Severus, the disciple and historian of saint Martin of Tours, informs us, that on one occasion, while accompanying this prelate on one of his pastoral visits, they heard of the faith and virtue of a christian virgin, who for many years had lived entirely isolated from the world. Her dwelling was in a small house, where none had admittance, save her attendant. St. Martin, notwithstanding his severe rule never to visit a female, thought that on this occasion he might depart from this rule, and honour, by a motive of religion, a person of such rare merit. Those who accompanied St. Martin, naturally thought that the recluse would be delighted to receive a visit from this renowned prelate; but to their great surprise, she declined the bishop's visit saying, by her attendant, that she could not deviate from the rules she had adopted; thus refusing to see her own bishop, who deigned to honour by his presence, her lowly cell. Sulpicius Severus makes the following reflections. " Who but " Saint Martin would not have considered this " refusal as a personal insult? Who but he would " not have felt displeased, even irritated ? Who " would not have indulged in resentful feelings?" The man of God, far from being offended at this refusal, quitted the recluse's dwelling with feelings of joy. Although he had not been allowed to see her, he spoke in the highest terms of her rare virtue, and was delighted to have met with one capable of giving an example, until then unknown in the country. Night having overtaken him, he remained in the neighbourhood. This circumstance enabled the recluse to send him different presents, which he accepted, saying: A bishop ought not to refuse offerings made by one, who should be preferred to many bishops. Sulpicius Severus thus concludes his remarks on this incident: " Let all know this " prodigy: a virgin consents not to be seen by Saint " Martin—a saint whom foreigners flocked to " see, and who was frequently visited by angels."

We may add, had the generous virtue of our Canadian heroine been known to Saint Martin, it would have elicited no smaller degree of admiration. We will even go so far as to say he would have bestowed still greater eulogiums upon her; viewing the heroic constancy she manifested, by remaining in her cell during the last moments of her departing mother.

Two years after our heroine's reclusion, her mother fell a prey to the disease which was soon to end her days. Strong natural claims of affection, strengthened by deep gratitude, bound Miss Le Ber to this fond parent; hence, what secret anguish must not have rent this loving daughter's bosom, when her dying mother's sobs reached her cell; but, knowing that she could in no-wise alleviate these sufferings which she so keenly felt; she assumed a calmness which differed vastly from her inward grief. She did not even quit her cell, to bestow the last proofs of filial love, on her dying parent. Her great submission to the decrees of Providence, even in the most trying circumstances, induced her to bear this severe trial, and to devote her time to earnest supplications to the Most High, for her mother's salvation, and restoration to health ; if, such would contribute to His glory : but divine wisdom willed it otherwise ; for Mrs. Le Ber died on the 8th of November 1682. The news of this sad event soon reached the cell of the holy recluse.   Although she had previously led a very austere life, her love for God had sweetened all the mortifications she had practised to crucify human nature, and to immolate herself entirely to him.   But the keenest and most cruel suffering she had to endure, that which pierced her heart in its most sensible and tender part, was the death of her fond mother : nevertheless, she withstood this severe trial with a fortitude worthy of her piety, and magnanimous courage.   Those loud lamentations, common on such occasions among persons of ordinary merit, were not witnessed in our heroine.   Without loosing for a moment, that holy peace which reigned within her soul; she adored the secret Judgments of God, and bowed beneath the stroke of his paternal hand with the most profound resignation.   Animated with celestial fortitude, she quits her cell, and enters her mother's apartment for the first time, since her seclusion.   Modestly approaching the bed of death she bends her knees in prayer, presses to her lips the hand of her departed mother, and bathes it with her tears ; then, without uttering a single word, although penetrated with most bitter sorrow, she leaves the apartment, and withdraws to her lonely cell.   There, in the presence of her God, she gives vent to her feelings; her tears come not from a desire of lightening the heavy burden, but that, united to fervent prayers and mortifications, they might appease God's Justice, and hasten for the departed soul, the moment of eternal bliss.

If young persons, can only admire Miss Le Ber's heroic fidelity, in remaining in her solitude under such very trying circumstances; all can imitate her sincere and generous charity, in endeavouring to deliver her mother's soul, from all sufferings in the other world. How many boast of their filial affection, and mourn, when death separates them from those they loved; yet, strange as it may appear, they scarcely breathe a fervent prayer for their eternal repose. Were these young persons true in their love, would they neglect this efficacious means of relieving departed souls? Should they not do all in their power to alleviate sufferings which are perhaps inflicted to expiate the excessive indulgence with which these parents treated them during life? Such young persons would dread the censure of the world, were they otherwise than clothed in mourning; lest they might be called heedless; the mere thought of such a thing awakens feelings of horror. They seem, however, to forget that true affection is not proved by a particular style of dress, or by wearing sombre-coloured garments, but by the dispositions of the heart, and by an earnest desire of procuring the eternal happiness of those we have loved. The use of mourning is doubtless a laudable custom, being an exterior mark of inward grief and of sincere affection; but when mourning is a mere exterior sign of feelings; it deceives the world, and even the deceased themselves, to whom this exterior garment, is nowise beneficial.

On perusing this chapter, many may consider Miss Le Ber's conduct as harsh and ungrateful; let them remember, that those alone, are ungrateful and hard-hearted, who neglect the most important of all duties, that of alleviating their parents' sufferings by prayers, and good works; or who, by remaining in a state of mortal sin, prevent these prayers from being beneficial to the departed. When persons voluntarily remain at enmity with God, they give evident proofs that they never had any real affection for their relatives, since they prefer their own gratification, which is both guilty and evanescent, to the eternal felicity of those from whom they are separated.

CHAPTER VI.

MISS LE BER PRONOUNCES A VOW OF PERPETUAL
SOLITUDE.—HER PURITY OF HEART AND
SPIRIT OF POVERTY.—HER CONDUCT AT
HER BROTHER'S DEATH.

As Miss Le Ber was an only daughter, it
seemed natural, that, after her mother's death, she
should take upon herself the various household
duties; and endeavour to console an afflicted father,
who had always lavished upon her, marks of the
fondest affection ; she might reasonably have taken
advantage of the various modifications, which had
been made, when she pronounced her vow ; and
would have been further justified in so doing, Mr.
Le Ber being left with three sons younger than
our heroine.   This event, far from disturbing our
recluse's manner of living, tended to inspire her
with an earnest desire of consummating her sacrifice, by embracing perpetual solitude, as the five
years of trial had elapsed.   Her hopes were soon
realized.

Her father took advantage of her being free, to

induce her to leave her solitude, and lead a less retired life, a consolation he might naturally expect from his only daughter, and Mr. Le Ber may have had plausible reasons, for requesting his daughter to take an active part in his household concerns, without neglecting her exercises of piety; her presence and conversation, would have enabled him to taste the sweetest enjoyments, which can be granted to a fond parent. But this self-sacrificing girl, thoroughly convinced that God required that she should lead a more perfect life, was far from abandoning her primitive fervour. She considered the happiness she had experienced during the five years of trial, and the benefits she had received during that time, as certain proofs that her sacrifice was agreeable to God; and instead of desiring the conversation, even of persons renowned for their piety; she secretly meditated some plan which would enable her to lead a still more solitary life, by absolute separation from the world.

During her years of trial, she had attended Mass and Vespers and other public offices, both on Sundays and holy-days. It is natural to suppose that a person so extraordinary, would attract unusual attention on account of her own virtue, and her father's social position. All eyes were turned upon her, and they deeply wounded her modesty for her sole desire was to live unknown. When the years of her probation had elapsed, she requested Mr. Seguenot, her Director, and Mr.

Dollier de Casson, Superior of the Seminary, to allow her to bind herself by a solemn vow, to the manner of living which she had heretofore followed. She also solicited the favour of being dispensed from attending any of the offices of the church; except first mass, when she received Holy Communion. She explained her reasons in such a persuasive manner, that her Directors, firmly convinced that God had inspired this desire, for the salvation of souls; at length, acceded to her request. When Mr. Le Ber was informed of her decision, he readily consented to it although he keenly felt the sundering of this last tie; but when convinced that God's glory and the edification of the colonists required it, he hesitated not, but willingly renounced the sweetness of his daughter's company, and agreed to live far from her, during the remainder of his life. This was undoubtedly the greatest sacrifice which a kind and virtuous father could make: Mr. Le Ber offered it to God with the exemplary generosity of a perfect Christian.

Miss Le Ber wished to consummate her sacrifice by taking a vow of perpetual seclusion. She chose for this purpose, the festival of Saint John the Baptist, June 24th 1685, and from that date, she felt a particular devotion to this great saint, whom she considered as the first holy hermit, and consequently, the model of all the solitaries of the New Law. This choice seems to indicate that the same spirit, which had led St. John to seek the desert, even in his childhood, had also inspired her.

The Spirit of God had led St. John, while yet a child, to quit the paternal roof and to retire to the desert, though exposed to no danger, while living with Saint Zachary and Saint Elizabeth; their examples could only tend to inculcate lessons of virtue; yet the holy precursor, faithful to what God required, remained in profound retreat; thus sacrificing the holiest and the greatest of consolations, that of beholding Jesus and of conversing with Him, for until our divine Lord had presented himself to be baptized by his hand, John had not yet beheld Him, as he himself informs us. Miss Le Ber took her vow on this day, that this sublime model might induce her to be faithful to her reclusion. Through obedience to her directors, she added, that her vow would be subject to the authority of her ecclesiastical superiors, so that they might be at liberty to introduce any modifications which prudence might suggest; and, which would be conformable to the rules followed by ancient recluses.

The vows of chastity and poverty were added to that of perpetual seclusion. The second was the most painful and the most meritorious; not on account of the impossibility of disposing of all her worldly goods, except as her director might think proper; but because she was not allowed to give up all, and to practise *real poverty*. Her father and her directors exacted this restriction, so that, at any future period she might be free to dispose of her property as God's glory would require. She humbly acquiesced in all that was required of her; and in after years, often acknowledged, that had this restriction not been made, she would most probably not have been enabled to realize many important designs, which contributed to glorify God.

This admirable solitary remained within her cell, not holding communication even with her relatives. She assisted at first mass with her attendant, but never quitted her reclusion to attend any of the other ceremonies of the Church, not even on the most solemn festivals.

She found a compensation for this sacrifice by uniting her prayers, to those of the faithful. As her chamber window was situated opposite to the sanctuary, she was enabled to hear all that was sung during Divine service. She thus enjoyed the advantage of raising her heart to God, with these pious chants, and could give vent to her fervour without attracting attention. During her hours of prayer, she turned towards the Church, and thus imitated Daniel, who was wont to turn towards the temple of Jerusalem. The adorable presence of Jesus Christ in the Blessed Sacrament, was the magnet which, attracted her towards the tabernacle, during all her exercises of piety, during her long and sublime meditations, both of the night and of the day: such was the strength and tenderness of her devotions, towards the blessed Eucharist.

Before embracing perpetual reclusion, she had

always adhered to the practice of kissing the floor in the Parish Church, both at the elevation of the Sacred Host, and before receiving Holy Communion; but having taken her vow, her confessor advised her to drop this custom. He doubtless thought, that as the decrease of fervour had induced the faithful to do away with this practice, our heroine's adhering to it might draw too much attention on her whose only desire was to remain hidden and unknown. Ill disposed people might have taxed her with singularity and condemned her mode of living; and he desired that she should be distinguished from others, only, by her modesty, and profound recollection.

Our heroine's wonderful humility added to her separation from the world; and the care she took to keep her attendant in total ignorance of her various practices of virtue, have doubtless deprived us of many edifying traits, which would have given additional interest to her admirable life. From the year 1685, when she took her vow of perpetual reclusion, until 1695, when she entered the Congregation de Notre Dame, she was seen but once, and that at the moment of her brother's tragical death. Her presence then produced the strongest impressions on the beholders, who were struck with that heroic virtue which she had previously practised at the death of her mother.

Mr. Jean Le Ber du Chesne's death occurred in the following manner. In the middle of August 1691, intelligence reached Ville Marie that 140

English, and 80 Indians were about to attack the town, and that they had already reached Lake Champlain. Mr. De Callière, then governor, immediately assembled both the regular troops and the militia, thus forming a body of about 1200 men. He then camped at the " Prairie de la Madeleine," where for the space of eight days he awaited the enemy. Seeing no signs of their approach, he attributed the delay to an attack on the Fort of Chambly, and therefore despatched Mr. de Vallerene in that direction with a detachment of eighty Canadians and eighty soldiers; the former commanded by Mr. Le Ber du Chesne, our heroine's brother.

The next day, Saturday, August the 11th, the enemy suddenly appearing an hour before the break of day, surprised the troops who had fallen asleep, and withdrew after having killed 30 men and wounded as many more. Mr. de Vallerene's detachment had gone but a short distance, when they heard the noise occasioned by the attack, and at once retraced their footsteps. About nine o'clock in the morning, as they were midway, between La Prairie and Chambly, they perceived the enemy approaching, and were attacked amidst the most fearful yells. On the enemy's first charge, Mr. de Vallerene ordered his men to conceal themselves behind a large fallen tree. His stratagem succeeded. They afterwards marched to meet the enemy, killed upwards of a hundred, and wounded many more. But the tree, which they had used as a rampart, was not large enough to protect all : five or six were wounded, and Mr. Le Ber du Chesne was among them.

He was at once brought to his father's house, where he died, in his twenty-third year, having received the rites of the church. He was buried on the 13th of August*. Sister Bourgeoys, accompanied by sister Barbier, hastened to this afflicted dwelling, in order to minister consolation to its sorrow-stricken inmates ; She also wished to embalm the body of the deceased. Miss Le Ber then quitted her cell, and remained with the nuns for a few minutes, not betraying the slightest weakness. The love she had ever entertained for her brother, did not even lead her to complain. She gave them what was necessary to lay out the body, but without uttering a word ; having prayed for some time, then retired to her cell. This conduct surprized and edified Sister Bourgeois, and her companion ; for they well knew in what true, merit consists ; and could appreciate fidelity to God, and heroic constancy in such trying circumstances.†

---

* An error was committed in Sister Bourgeoys' life relating to the day on which the skirmish which proved fatal to Mr. Le Ber took place ; it is spoken of as having occurred on the 3rd of August.

† According to the custom prevalent among the natives, an Indian prisoner was given to Mr. Le Ber to replace the son whom he had lost.

The following day, August the 14th, Mr. Le Ber, his daughter, and one of his sons, (these were probably his only children residing in Ville Marie), performed an action truly worthy of the profound religious feeling, which had ever animated them, and which also served as a memorial of their noble minds. Knowing that the deceased had intended to assist Mr. Francis Charron in carrying out his design, for the establishment of the General Hospital for the poor of the town, they employed a notary to draw up an act, whereby they gave a farm for this purpose at Point St. Charles, with all its dependencies, "in order," said they, to carry out the desire manifested by the late John Le Ber du Chesne."

This farm covered an area of about 35 acres, which were included in the concessions belonging to John de Saint Père and to Nicholas Godé, who had been cruelly put to death on that spot by the Iroquois in 1657. That property had been given to Mr. le Ber in 1661 by the proprietors of the Island. The donation made by Mr. Le Ber and his children in favour of the General Hospital, was accepted by Mr. Guyotte of the Seminary of Saint Sulpice, who was then officiating as parish priest. Provision was made in the contract, that should this design not be carried out, the revenue of the farm should be always employed in succouring the poor of Ville Marie. Miss Le Ber and her brother Peter, of whom we shall shortly speak, signed this act, to prove that they agreed with their father.

As Miss Le Ber had submitted her rule of silence to her director, he probably advised her to communicate with persons of note, who were very desirous of knowing her opinion on some points. This supposition arises from the fact that Mr. Tronson informs us of, in 1693, Mr. De La Colombière wishing to re-enter the Seminary of Saint Sulpice, which he had voluntarily quitted, visited Miss Le Ber, and had a long conversation with her, which did not produce the desired result. Although our admirable heroine lived in entire seclusion, her manner of living did not satisfy her heart's most ardent desire, that of being still more retired. It was with feelings of piety, that she daily repaired to the Parish Church for first mass, at which she often received Holy Communion: but her happiness would have been complete, had it been possible for her to enjoy the same privileges without leaving her cell. During nearly fourteen years she mourned in secret over the imperfect solitude in which she dwelt; but after that lapse of time, God was pleased to grant the fulfilment of her desires, as shall be related in the following book.

BOOK THIRD.

MISS LE BER ENTERS THE CONVENT OF THE
CONGREGATION DE NOTRE-DAME, HER
LOVE AND DEVOTION TOWARDS THE
BLESSED SACRAMENT.

CHAPTER I.

MISS LE BER WISHES TO ENTER THE CONVENT
OF THE CONGREGATION DE NOTRE-DAME,
THERE TO LIVE IN ENTIRE RECLUSION.

Although the privilege of having the Blessed
Sacrament beneath her roof had been sister Bourgeoys' most ardent desire, since the foundation of
her community; still, her profound veneration for
the adorable presence of our Lord in this mystery, prevented her requesting the Ecclesiastical
superiors to grant this favor, on account of the
diminutive size of the oratory, and its proximity
to the other apartments. She however finally

agreed with the Nuns on this point, and resolved
to build a church in the garden alongside the
buildings occupied by the community ; this church
was to be 54 feet long, and 26 feet broad;
constructed in such a manner that it might
be a fit dwelling for our Lord. The preliminary
arrangements were made in the spring of 1694,
and the workmen agreed to finish the masonry
before the end of the following July. As this
determination interested all pious souls ; Miss
Le Ber soon heard of it, the news rejoiced her,
as it led her to hope that she might one
day take up her abode near this new church,
and there enjoy the happiness for which her soul
languished ; that of worshipping the Blessed Sacrament with her wonted fervour, without quitting
her reclusion. Many motives induced her to choose
this abode ; the veneration she had always
entertained towards sister Bourgeoys and her
companions, the strong impressions of grace
produced upon her by their example,—for to
them did she attribute her perseverance in her
retired mode of life ; the inestimable privilege of
living and dying in an institution so specially consecrated to the Blessed Virgin seemed to promise
the realisation of her fondest hopes. Her spiritual
director Mr. Seguenot, and her father, in no way
opposed it, and allowed her to give the amount necessary to finish the new church in which she
wished her cell to be placed, and where she desired
to end her days. She therefore communicated her

plan to the sisters of the Congregation, and expressed her desire of assisting them, if they would receive her in their institution, not to follow their rules, but to be considered as one of the sisterhood, and be henceforth known, as sister Le Ber.

The Sisters of the Congregation had ever regarded this favoured soul as a prodigy of grace; hence, they were delighted at the prospect of being thus enabled to contribute to God's Glory, to the edification of the colonists, and to the complete happiness of this child of predilection. Secondary considerations also induced them to comply with her request: veneration for the Blessed Sacrament had led them to undertake, what worldly prudence condemned; their funds being very low, owing to the money lately expended in erecting the buildings then occupied by the Community. They consequently accepted Miss Le Ber's proposal with gratitude, and agreed that she should make such arrangements as she might think proper; adding, that she would be at liberty to choose and place her cell in whatever manner she would deem most suitable.

Miss Le Ber wished that the general appearance of the church of the Congregation should resemble, as much as possible, the holy house of Nazareth, wherein the great mystery of the Incarnation had been accomplished, and which is now seen in the Cathedral of Loretto in Italy. This revered dwelling is of an oblong shape: a slight partition encloses that part so respectfully visited by pilgrims,

and known as the Holy Chamber; this is entered
by two doors, one on the right, the other on the
left; the altar is placed in the most spacious part
of the chapel between the two doors. It was
Miss Le Ber's desire that the new church should
be erected on a similar plan, that a small space
should be reserved behind the altar to form a cell
about 10 or 12 feet in depth, including the width
of the church; she drew up the following plan for
this particular part of the Church.

It was to be divided into three stories, reserving
the second and third for her own use; the first,
situated on the ground floor was to be used as a
vestry. She proposed to descend to this apartment
to receive Holy Communion, and to go to Confession; for this purpose, she desired that one of the
panels of the door on the Gospel side, should be
replaced by a moveable grating; behind which she
might kneel, to receive Holy Communion without'
being seen, and go to Confession without quitting
her cloister, or her confessor entering her apartment.
Another door opened on the Nuns' garden, so
that her food might be brought to her this way, and
not through the church.

Her proximity to the Blessed Sacrament was the
advantage she most highly prized : nought but a
slight partition was to separate her from the dwelling of the Loved Spouse of her heart. The plan
had been so laid out, that her humble couch might
be on a line with the Blessed Sacrament, in whose
immediate vicinity she was henceforth to dwell.

This thought filled her with a pure and holy joy,
or rather, it caused her heart to dissolve in feelings
of the most lively, and tender gratitude.

The third story was to be her laboratory wherein she might keep articles she used in working.

CHAPTER II.

EXAMINATION OF MISS LE BER'S VOCATION.
THE CEREMONY OF HER SOLEMN RECLUSION.

Although fifteen years had elapsed, since Miss
Le Ber had first embraced the solitary mode of
life, in which she had so zealously persevered, to the
great edification of the faithful; still her reclusion
could not be considered, as sanctioned by Ecclesiastical authorities, such as had formerly been the
case with recluses of the primitive ages; no public
ceremony had solemnized her first vow of reclusion
for five years, nor even her final vow : her director's
approbation had been the sole sanction she had
sought. These considerations led Mr. Dollier de
Casson, Superior of the Seminary of Ville Marie,
and Vicar General of the Bishop, who was then
in France, to think that her entire separation from
the world, should be accompanied with due solemnity:
and thus, be quite conformable to ancient discipline,
and at the same time, prove advantageous to Religion. He therefore examined Miss Le Ber's vocation, in order to ascertain her dispositions towards

embracing perpetual reclusion; but this examination was a mere formality, for that love of retirement which she had manifested during fifteen years,
and her fidelity to all her promises, had impressed
all so strongly, that no one entertained the least
doubt concerning her calling to this manner of
living, and her perseverance in it until her last
breath.   Mr. Dollier, being administrator of the
diocese, authentically approved Miss Le Ber's vocation by sanctioning, and by choosing the 5th of
August for the solemn ceremony of her reclusion;
he also approved the agreement made between our
heroine and the Sisters of the Congregation, previous to her retiring into their institution.

The original document may still be seen in the
Prothonotary's office in Montreal, as drawn up by
a notary called Basset.   We cannot refrain from
inserting the most striking passages, for it is a precious memorial of Miss Le Ber.

" Miss Jane Le Ber, being desirous of dwelling
" in retirement, so long as God will be pleased to give
" her the grace requisite to do so; had recourse
" to the secular Nuns of the Congregation de Notre
" Dame established at Ville Marie, they, having
" acceded to her proposal; she consents to defray
" the greater part of the expense incurred by build-
" ing the chapel, situated in their grounds and a
" small apartment built behind the chapel.   She
" has chosen this spot for her abode, and is now
" about to take possession of it.

" Wishing to agree with the Nuns, as to what

' they would allow for her maintenance, Mr.
" Dollier de Casson, Superior of the Seminary of
" this Town and Vicar General of the diocese, has
" sanctioned the following agreement : The Nuns
" will supply her with food and fuel both in sick-
" ness and in health; and this is to be continued
" as long as she thinks proper.

" The Nuns also bind themselves to board Anna
" Barroy, Miss Le Ber's cousin, who will remain
" in the Community as long as she desires, and,
" should she be absent, Miss Le Ber will be waited
" upon by the Sisters themselves.

" In consideration of the aforesaid services, Miss
" Le Ber gives the Sisters of the Congregation de
" Notre Dame the funds they received from her
" for the building of the chapel, to which she adds
" the money she may expend in decorating and
" supplying it with ornaments and sacred vessels.
" She also grants them the annual pension of 500
" livres, French coin, reserving 75 livres worth of
" wool, or silk, or other materials which she may
" require for needle work.

" In return for the gift, thus bestowed upon the
" Nuns, by Miss Le Ber's generous contribution to
" the construction of the chapel; they bind them-
" selves to pray for the repose of her soul, and for
" the souls of her relatives."

This act was signed by Sister Barbier, Superioress of the Congregation de Notre Dame, by the
principal members of the Community, and by Mr.
Dollier de Casson.

At length on the 5th of August, feast of "Notre Dame des Neiges," which, in 1695, fell on a Friday, Vespers having been sung, the faithful who had assisted, formed a procession and followed the clergy who left the parish Church for Mr. Le Ber's dwelling, in order to conduct this innocent virgin to her new abode; she was destined to be offered in expiation for the sins of many, and could certainly be looked upon as a victim immolated to God's glory.

She was found absorbed in prayer, and wholly engrossed with the happiness of consummating her sacrifice, by embracing perpetual reclusion. On beholding her, all were struck with her unassuming modesty. She wore a woollen gown, with a veil and head dress resembling those worn by the Nuns of the Congregation, but differing in color. Her dress was of a greyish white, confined to the waist by a black belt; she had chosen this peculiar color, the better to imitate Mary, her glorious model, for she knew that the Blessed Virgin had once appeared to sister Bourgeoys in a similar garment, as is related in the life of the holy foundress. She wore a belt as a symbol of penance, and to remind her that she differed vastly from that spotless Virgin who was Immaculate in her Conception; it also called to mind that although original guilt had been effaced by Baptism, her duty as a Christian, required that she should avenge Divine Justice by leading a mortified and penitential life.

She quitted for ever the home of her childhood,

and followed the clergy accompanied by her virtuous father and several relatives, who had been
invited to witness the most touching ceremony that
had ever taken place in Ville Marie. The procession
moved towards the church of the Congregation,
while appropriate hymns were sung. All the citizens had assembled to look on this unusual scene,
and few could refrain from shedding tears, on beholding this innocent virgin about to enter an abode,
which might be considered as her tomb. Her social
position tended to heighten the interest of the beholders; being the wealthiest heiress in Canada,
among the great ones of earth, she could have chosen
a brilliant position in the world; yet, she generous
ly spurned all worldly goods and pleasures, to obtain
a more estimable treasure.

Her plain and simple style of dress, the innocence
and mildness that illumined her countenance, her
firm yet unassuming bearing, and the sight of that
virtuous father, who seemed to lead the victim to the
place of sacrifice; also contributed to awaken deep
emotions in the hearts of all present. This was
undoubtedly the most signal victory that Faith
had obtained, over the worldly spirit which had
already manifested itself in this country. Astonishment arose in every mind on thus beholding
innocence and mortification, subdue that love of
pleasure so inherent to our nature—all wondered
on seeing that in our heroine, voluntary poverty
and a love of solitude triumphed over attachment
to the transitory enjoyments of the riches of this

world, and over those passions which so often rule us; but the greatest of all victories, was that of Divine Love over filial affection; this could certainly be termed the triumph of Faith over reason, and of Grace over nature. This victory was rendered still more complete, on beholding parental love, humbly bow before the light of Faith, and willingly submit to the decrees of the Almighty.

Angels might have admired the generosity which Mr. Le Ber evinced in mastering the anguish he experienced. He would have bestowed a large dower on his daughter, had she remained in the world; yet, in this trying circumstance, he voluntarily sacrificed the consolation he would have received, had she dwelt with him, to minister to his wants, and be the consolation of his declining years. The struggle between duty and affection was so very strong, he was so fondly attached to his daughter, that none attributed his calmness to indifference, for he left the church of the Congregation, as soon as the procession reached it; he dared not remain during the ceremony, lest excessive grief should cause exhaustion.

After his departure, Mr. Dollier, who presided, blessed the recluse's new cell, and addressed her, as she humbly knelt before him, surrounded by the clergy, by the Nuns of the Congregation de Notre Dame, and by the faithful who had assembled to witness the ceremony. He exhorted her to persevere in her retired dwelling as zealously as Magdalen had persevered in her grotto; then led her to her chamber in which she enclosed herself, while the choir sung the litany of the Blessed Virgin.

The following day, being the feast of the Transfiguration of Our Lord, Mr. Dollier offered up the first mass in this chapel; Mr. Le Ber assisted at it; his presence seemed to indicate that he wished to atone for the weakness manifested on the previous day, and to prove that he was willing to ratify the sacrifice he had offered to God.

CHAPTER III.

Mr. Dollier de Casson thus speaks of Mr. Le
Ber's generosity, in the following extract from the
act of the sister Le Ber's reclusion.

" I blessed the chapel on the 6th of August, and
" celebrated Mass which was accompanied by the
" best singing that could be heard in Canada; the
" church was intensely crowded, and Mr. Le Ber
" was present. On the previous day he had brought
" his loved and only daughter to the Convent of
" the Congregation; but, paternal fondness had
" prevented him from assisting at the ceremony of
" her reclusion; to-day however he proved that
" notwithstanding the depth of his affection, he
" was willing that his daughter, his sweetest conso-
" lation, should be consecrated to God, to contri-
" bute to His glory, and to the edification of the
" colony; he offered himself to the Almighty for
" the same purpose. Two victims have thus been
" sacrificed to God in that hallowed sanctuary;

" there, dwells the daughter, and there also, are cen-
" tered the affections of a father left alone in the
" world, in the 64th year of his age."

We cannot refrain praising the astonishing
magnanimity which Mr. Le Ber displayed:
strong indeed, must have been the ties which bound
this father to his daughter; these ties had been
strengthened during his widowhood, and she was
his only child.

The scene in which he acted such a prominent
part, must have reminded the beholders of that
witnessed by Abraham's followers, when the Patri-
arch led Isaac towards the place of sacrifice. True
it is, that he was weighed down by excessive anguish, and that parental love could ill repress its
outbursts; the brave warrior, who had so often exposed his life in defence of his country, lacked
sufficient courage to be a calm witness of the touching ceremony, during which his cherished daughter
had consecrated herself irrevocably to God. The
Almighty, doubtless allowed that this should happen,
to prove the extent of Mr. Le Ber's sacrifice; had
this incident not occurred, many might have
underrated his merit.

Abraham's sacrifice, was limited to his interior
acquiescence to the orders of the Almighty, his son
returned with him, full of life and health; yet his
submission had been so agreeable to the Almighty,
that he was selected as the father of God's chosen
people; and his reward was not confined to the
present, he was told that from his posterity all

nations would be blessed, and even the Messiah would be born of his race. Whence came such special blessings? From the fact, that he had conquered nature's claims when strongest, and had made them yield to the decrees of God: this fidelity seemed to be a harbinger of the annihilation of his race; yet, it entitled him to the celebrity which has since been attached to his name.

We are induced to think, that Mr. Le Ber's generosity was rewarded in a similar manner; for the sacrifice which he made by offering his only daughter to the Almighty, and allowing her to embrace perpetual reclusion, tended to immortalize his name, and not to bury it in oblivion, as many had expected. Hence, some years later, Mr. de Belmont was heard to say: " The Le Ber family " occupies a distinguished position in Canada, and " we may fearlessly add that Miss Le Ber imparted " a new lustre to her race." Truly has her name been handed down to posterity, encircled by a bright halo of virtuous actions which differs vastly from that notoriety which other names have obtained; far from sinking into oblivion, it will be repeated throughout future ages; then, as now, it will awaken recollections; of one, whose sweet and winning qualities rendered her a fit model for young persons, in all positions of life; of one, who was a prodigy of virtue, and Canada's fairest ornament; it may also remind Christian parents, that they should imitate Mr. Le Ber's spirit of self sacrifice.

For as Miss Le Ber can be given as a model of

H

that fidelity with which all young persons should persevere in their respective callings, her worthy father's example should inculcate an important lesson on the minds of many parents; that, of endeavouring to fulfil God's designs on their children, by affording them all available means of sanctifying themselves in the state of life to which they are called.

Too many have unfortunately neglected this sacred duty, little did they think, their eternal happiness was closely connected with its faithful accomplishment; being deluded by their natural inclinations, parental fondness obtained complete mastery over them; when Faith should have guided, and taught them, to love the Divine Giver, more firmly than His gifts. Some, parental love led to induce their children to disobey God, when nought but love of self, or personal interest had been the source of this selfish conduct. We shall mention a well-known trait wherein this is clearly proved; it may impress our readers with a more profound feeling of admiration of that pure and high minded affection which Mr. Le Ber entertained for his only daughter.

During the persecution that raged under the emperor Severus, Vivia Perpetua, a noble Carthaginian lady of 22 years of age, was seized and brought to prison. She thus related her father's conduct during her imprisonment.

" While my companions were undergoing an " examination, my father made his appearance,

" holding my babe in his arms,—he drew me aside,
" and begged me to have mercy on my child
" The judge perceived that he wished to draw me
" still further away, and ordered him to be expelled ;
" some one struck him with a rod, and I felt the
" blow more keenly than if I had myself received
" it, for, I was heart-broken on seeing my
" father so cruelly treated in his old age. Shortly
" afterwards he came to the prison, and seemed to
" labor under a heavy burden. My daughter, said
" he, take pity on my grey hairs, take pity on thy
" father; spurn me not from thee, nor render
" me a despicable being, for I have watched over
" thee till now, and loved thee more than I loved
" thy brothers. Behold thy mother and thy aunt,
" behold thy infant son, whose life depends on
" thine. Affection, doubtless prompted this lan-
" guage, my father then wept bitterly, he knelt
" before me and no longer called me daughter, but
" lady. He paid frequent visits to the prison ;
" he came to see me before the day appointed for
" the execution, on this occasion, he pulled his
" beard through anger, he writhed on the ground,
" cursed himself, and uttered the most appalling
" threats."

This proves what tyrannical sway self-love can
exert over some parents: this unfortunate father
loved himself, and not his daughter. His partiality
towards her, proceeded from his fondness for himself, he it was whom he idolized in her ; a desire of
selfish enjoyment induced him to do all in his

L. of C.

power to prevent her martyrdom. It mattered not to him whether his daughter wished to sacrifice her life, or whether all her relatives considered martyrdom as the greatest blessing, he was opposed to it because it inflicted a deep wound on his selfish fondness. Saint Perpetua adds. " I pitied him " on account of the inflexible obduracy he mani- " fested at such an advanced time of life ; and he " was the only member of the family, who did not " rejoice at the prospect of my martyrdom."

This deluded father also feared that his daughter's fidelity to Christ might bring shame on himself ; he therefore availed himself of all practicable means to induce her to abjure the tenets of the Christian faith. The thought that he grieved and injured his daughter by treating her in this most inhuman manner, never restrained him ; yet, had he succeeded in rendering her an apostate, he would have deprived her of that peace of heart which is man's greatest treasure ; she would have scandalized the faithful ; her conduct would have awakened feelings of horror and disgust within the heart of those, who had boldly confessed their belief ; hell would have triumphed, while the Church would have mourned, and the Almighty would have spurned her from Him, as an apostate and rebellious servant, as a perjurer and a declared enemy. He proved how selfishness ruled him and mastered parental love, when he went so far as to strike his daughter ; his threats and entreaties having proved alike abortive, he was so indignant when she persisted in saying she was a Christian, that according to her own account: " My perseverance irritated my father, " and provoked him to such a degree, that he in- " tended to put out my eyes; but he retired satis- " fied with having ill-treated me,—and in despair at " the thought of having been conquered." The shameful conduct of this deluded father naturally awakens feelings of horror within all Christian souls, yet similar examples have sometimes been witnessed among those, who style themselves Christian parents; parents pretend to try their children's vocation, and this so called ordeal, is nought but a most strenuous and oft-repeated endeavour to win their youthful hearts from God, and to centre their affections on the allurements of the world. The persecution which Saint Perpetua's father waged against his child, inspired her with renewed perseverance; her courage remained undaunted, even when parental love turned to frensy; such however, is unfortunately not the usual result of those perfidious means used to inspire children with a taste for pleasure; fatal consequences too often ensue, and this inordinate and selfish love which St. Perpetua's father evinced, is the cause of all these misfortunes. Many parents love their offspring from selfish motives and endeavour to enliven old age, by inducing their children to partake of those enjoyments which can be theirs no longer; hence, some parents create difficulties when their children wish to avoid sin, and express a praiseworthy desire of living according to the maxims of the Gospel;

others exert all their influence to prevent any one
of their children from embracing a religious life;
should they finally consent, they neglect no means
of retarding the event; but if the same child sought
to occupy a distinguished position in the world,
no means of ensuring success would be neglected,
inexperience would not be thought of, and that
extreme youth so loudly condemned when young
persons choose the better part, would be a very
secondary condition, if a high social position could
be secured. When parents act thus, it is quite
evident that the world rules them, and that God has
but a small share in their affections; hence, it is
that no satisfaction, and no eagerness are evinced
when a religious life is chosen; some parents are
so selfish, as to force their children to remain in
the world, and thus run the risk of exposing their
eternal welfare.

Mr. Le Ber's conduct differed vastly from this
unchristian behaviour: he proved the sincerity of
the affection he bore his daughter, by sacrificing his
happiness, to ensure hers. Being highly esteemed
by the colonists, his pure and disinterested way of
acting, exerted a most beneficial influence over
many fathers; from this date a great increase of
members was witnessed in the religious communities of Ville Marie; the colony was then enabled
to supply its own wants. Nought, but the happy
results effected by Miss Le Ber's example, could
equal those produced by that of her father; the
graces attendant upon her sacrifice were so striking,

that when Mr. de Belmont delivered her panegyric, he mentioned this well-known fact and thus spoke to the Sisters of the Congregation de Notre-Dame: " Sister Le Ber's example has drawn down special " blessings on many souls ; it has re-echoed within " the hearts of many virgins who are present at " this ceremony, and who are indebted to her for " their vocation."

CHAPTER IV.

OUR HEROINE'S EXAMPLE INDUCED HER BROTHER TO LEAD A PERFECT LIFE.

Mr. Peter Le Ber's edifying life, was one of the most signal graces, which our heroine's reclusion drew down upon the colony; his estimable sister's example so touched his heart, that he resolved to embrace a perfect life, and joined Mr. Francis Charon de la Barre, in the hopes of founding the institution of the Hospital Friars in Ville Marie; he and his brother Mr. Le Ber du Chesne, were its most distinguished benefactors.

When he heard that his sister intended to defray a great part of the expense, incurred in the building of the church of the Congregation de Notre-Dame; he wished to be a sharer in this good work, by supplying all the stone required. Mr. Peter Le Ber had always manifested true filial affection towards the Blessed Virgin and towards Saint Ann, for whom he entertained a peculiar devotion; he also sought to propagate this devotion. Seeing, that Sister Bourgeoys had erected a chapel in honor of Our Lady of Bonsecours, some distance out of town, that the faithful might repair thither on pilgrimages, and processions stop there, he wished to build one in honor of Saint Ann in the other extremity of the town. Mr. Dollier de Casson sanctioned this pious design, and granted an acre of ground situated at point Saint Charles; the chapel was at once erected, and Mass celebrated for the first time on the 17th of November, 1698. Hence, comes the name of Saint Ann's given to this part of the city. The pilgrimages made by several of the faithful, and the offices which were sometimes celebrated in this chapel, certainly tended to increase and even to popularize devotion towards the mother of our Blessed Lady. Mr. Le Ber also manifested his piety, by painting several pictures for this chapel, and by bestowing a certain amount of money on the Seminary of Saint-Sulpice, in order to defray the expenses necessary to keep the chapel in order; but being isolated from the town, after the conquest of Canada by the British, it was very much exposed, and even, on several occasions, the doors and windows were shattered. The priests of the Seminary therefore thought it prudent to have it demolished, so that similar profanations might not again occur; intending, however to rebuild it when circumstances would allow their doing so. Hence, shortly afterwards when Mr. Montgolfier wrote Miss Le Ber's life, he said; " More favorable circumstances may " doubtless enable the faithful to renew this devo- " tion." This design was executed some years since: the priests of the Seminary raised an edifice in the same part of the town, and the Bishop of Montreal solemnly re-established the well-known pilgrimage. The better to awaken the piety of the faithful, this revered Prelate himself repaired to the Church daily, during the octave of Saint Ann's feast; his example was followed by the various religious congregations of the city; the members of these orders united in pilgrimages; and other pious citizens joined so eagerly, that it awakened recollections of the fervour which had animated the first colonists.

Mr. Peter Le Ber took as much interest in the rising institution of the Congregation de Notre-Dame, as his sister; he therefore willed that the sisters of the Congregation, should receive the revenue of a sum of 10,000 livres. His devotion to the Blessed Virgin and to her mother was such, that he laid down as a condition, that one of the Nuns, should bear the name of Saint Mary and another that of Saint Ann. This fervent Christian died at Point Saint Charles, on the 1st of October, 1707; his remains were interred in the church of the Hospital-Friars, now known as that of the Hotel-Dieu, and are still there at the present day. In accordance with his dying request, his heart was placed in the church of the Congregation, where his sister dwelt in reclusion. We are inclined to think, that even after death, he wished to be united in spirit to that pious sister, in order to participate in the merit and fervour of her prayers.

CHAPTER V.

MISS LE BER'S DEVOTION TOWARDS THE BLESSED
SACRAMENT. TWO ENGLISH GENTLEMEN
VISIT HER.

Sister Le Ber's life, from her reclusion in the
Convent of the Congregation de Notre-Dame, until
her death, can be truly called a ceaseless homage
rendered unto Jesus present in this Sacrament of
love. This innocent virgin, may be compared to
a lamp ever burning before Him, or rather to a heavenly perfume, daily consuming itself in the Divine
Presence. Immediately after High Mass which
had been celebrated the day following that of her
solemn reclusion, the Blessed Sacrament was exposed for the first time, during forty hours in the
chapel of the Congregation. Sister Bourgeois, as
well as the entire sisterhood, had long solicited this
favour, and these fervent souls looked forward with
heartfelt delight, to the moment when they would
possess the Blessed Sacrament, beneath their
roof; yielding to the impulse of their grateful love
towards Jesus, in His adorable Sacrament; they

could not conceal their feelings, yet none among them experienced that pure and holy joy which filled sister Le Ber's soul; for her withdrawal to the Convent seemed to have attracted thither the Spouse of Virgins. Her profound retreat in rear of the Tabernacle, also seemed to indicate that she was the chosen object of the rarest favours and choicest blessings. She enjoyed the great happiness of living in the immediate vicinity of the Divine Eucharist; nought, but a slight partition separated her from it, and when she indulged in a few short hours of sleep, her head rested within a few inches of the Tabernacle; hence, her stay in this cherished cell, was an uninterrupted communication with her heart's beloved. Although she honored Him by numerous exercises of piety, and daily consecrated three and sometimes five hours to mental prayer; all her occupations afforded her means of communing with that Jesus who dwelt so near her. True it is, that her actions differed one from the other, but her feelings of interior union with Jesus remained unchangeable; they resembled streams in different countries, yet, bearing the same waters throughout. Her life was one protracted mental prayer, a ceaseless, heavenward ascension towards Jesus; an unbroken union with His adorable person. Her bodily position also proved how strongly she was attached to Jesus truly present in the Blessed Sacrament; for not only did she turn towards the Tabernacle during her exercises of piety, and while assisting at the Holy Sacrifice,

but also, during her most ordinary actions, such as
her meals, which she always took on her knees;
the charms which drew her towards her heart's beloved, were far stronger than the attraction which
draws the loadstone towards the poles.   These circumstances enable us to form a slight conception
of the celestial love, which must have burned with
in her, when about to receive Him, whom Faith
had taught her to adore unceasingly.   She enjoyed
this happiness four times each week.   The days of
Holy Communion must have been days of heavenly
delight, and transports of seraphic joy to her, whose
heart was so ardently inflamed with love for Jesus;
this sacred flame so burned within her, that the day
seemed not long enough to satisfy her heart's
yearnings; she willingly sacrificed hours of sleep,
and arose regularly at midnight, to commune with
her Heavenly Spouse.   She feared not to enter the
chapel when silence reigned around; knowing that
all the members of the Community were then
wrapped in slumber, she was wont to repair to the
chapel, prostrate herself on the steps of the altar, and
remain there an entire hour in silent adoration;
the most intense cold never diminished her fervour;
on the vigils of feasts, her meditation lasted two
hours.   Then it was that she united her homage
to that rendered unto Jesus by the Holy Angels
who unceasingly surround our Tabernacles: this
was one of her favorite occupations.   She also
oined the Heavenly Spirits, in their praises of the
Blessed Trinity, saying with them: Holy, holy,

holy is the God of hosts, the heaven and the earth are filled with His glory. She often repeated the doxology, Glory be to the Father, and to the Son, and to the Holy Ghost : as it was in the beginning, is now, and ever shall be, world without end. Amen. She also offered herself unceasingly to the Almighty, as an expiatory victim, for the crimes of sinners, by uniting her oblation to that of Jesus, the Sacred Lamb, who was slain for the sins of the world, and who is the only propitiatory offering we can present to the Father. The better to succeed in identifying herself with this Sacred Victim ; she sought to become united to Mary, who shared so largely in His sacrifice on Calvary, and who now glorified in Heaven, still intercedes for all sinners.

As Jesus, truly present in the adorable Sacra ment, was the sole object of our heroine's affection so was He the sole aim of the ordinary actions which she performed between her exercises of piety. She worked continually for Jesus, excepting when the poor required her assistance. As her cell was a representation of the holy house of Nazareth, she remembered that Mary had prepared the linen and garments that the Child Jesus wore ; and willingly endeavoured to participate in the dispositions which had animated this Immaculate Mother, knowing that the linen and other articles, which she made would come in contact with Our Lord's sacred body, and that the vestments and altar fronts, which she adorned so tastefully, would also contribute to His glory and to the magnificence of His temples. On entering the Convent of the Congregation, she had expressed a desire of contributing to the decoration of the new church, and of furnishing some of the vestments which might be required. This promise was eagerly and generously kept; for she made almost all the vestments that were used during her lifetime, and kindly purchased what she could not make. She gave a very handsome Tabernacle, a Ciborium, a Chalice, an Ostensorium, and a Lamp, made of silver and very delicately worked; these objects may still be seen at the Congregation. Villa-Maria has the honor and highly esteemed privilege of possessing the Ostensorium bestowed by Miss Le Ber, as also an altar vestment which she embroidered.

Although she offered these exterior gifts to Jesus they did not satisfy her ardent love; neither was she contented with the interior homage she rendered unto Him; she therefore requested Sister Bourgeoys and her companions to join her in making arrangements to establish the Perpetual Adoration. This proposal was willingly and joyfully accepted and sister Le Ber's desire gratified, so that excepting certain days, when the Blessed Sacrament was exposed at the Parish church, one of the sisters was in constant adoration before the Tabernacle; offering up the prayers of the entire Community. The better to ensure fidelity to this holy practice, so that Our Lord should always receive this tribute presented by fervent souls Miss Le Ber desired that the Sisters of the Congregation should bind themselves to follow it, and offered them a gift of 3,000 livres for this purpose. They accepted the offer with feelings of gratitude and Mr. Dollier de Casson gave his approbation to the pious and useful offering. As she wished Our dear Lord to be duly honoured in this church, she made arrangements that the Holy Sacrifice of the Mass might be there offered daily by a priest of the Seminary, at whatever hour the Nuns might appoint, assigning 8,000 livres to defray the expenses attendant on this observance.

As ardent love for the Blessed Sacrament induced Sister Le Ber to embrace this secluded life, it also led her to practice those austere mortifications and voluntary privations, which she daily inflicted upon herself. Mgr. de Saint Valier, bishop of Quebec, visited the Convent of the Congregation on his return from France in 1698, and was highly gratified on beholding the edifying recluse, of whom report said so much. He visited her in her cell and was astonished at her manner of living; he also admired the strength of mind, the generosity and the heroic constancy of this favoured soul.

Two English gentlemen of rank who happened to be in Ville Marie at the time, and were acquainted with the Le Ber family, made known to the Bishop the desire they entertained of seeing this famous recluse, in order to judge of the correctness of the wonderful statements made concerning her. The prelate, firmly convinced that the sight of this angelic being would produce a most salutary impression on the strangers, accompanied them himself to her cell. They could not express their amazement on beholding Canada's wealthiest daughter in such an abject abode, and deprived of most of the necessaries of life; for although sister Le Ber retained the right of disposing of her fortune, she practised poverty as rigorously as a fervent religious could do in the most austere orders; hence, they were greatly astonished on seeing her clothed in a coarse woollen garment, with an apron of similar material, and wearing coarse straw shoes, made, by herself, of the husks of Indian corn. Her couch also attracted their attention, it was composed of a simple straw bed; a bundle of the same material sufficed for her pillow; she never slept on a mattrass nor used any other covering but a coarse blanket. Her food was as simple as her dress and couch, for although she was too delicate to abstain from meat her repasts were as frugal as they could possibly be; she took boiled meat for dinner, and soup for supper; but on Saturdays and the vigils of several feasts, her only nourishment was bread and water.

These strangers could not conceal their astonishment. One of them, a protestant minister, asked why she led such an abject life, when she might have partaken of the greatest enjoyments that the world could offer. She replied: "A magnet has "drawn me hither, and keeps me thus separated "from all the luxuries of life." The other gentleman wished to know what this magnet could be. They were on the ground floor, Miss Le Ber opened the window through which she always received Holy Communion, humbly kneeling, she cast a glance towards the altar, and said: " Behold the " magnet ;" Our Lord truly present in the Divine " Eucharist; He it is who induced me to renounce " all else to enjoy the happiness of dwelling near " Him. No power on earth, could sever the bands " which unite me to my God."

She then spoke of this august mystery with such a lively faith, such an ardent zeal, and in tones of such passionate love for God, that the minister was quite confounded. Sister Le Ber was endowed with great fluency of speech ; religious convictions were so strongly impressed on her mind and heart, that when she conversed on any pious subject, she truly seemed inspired from above. Her faith in the dogma of the Real Presence, and the incomprehensible love God evinces therein towards man, tended to inflame her ardour; and on this occasion, she produced strong impressions on her visitors. Upon his return home, the Protestant minister often related the circumstances of, this visit: he spoke of sister Le Ber as a prodigy . and as the greatest wonder that Canada possessed. We are indebted to Mr. de Belmont for the foregoing facts. About fifty years after sister Le Ber's death, Mr. Montgolfier, superior of the Seminary of Ville-Marie, said he had been informed that this minister subsequently abjured heretical doctrines to embrace the true Faith. The life sister Le Ber led in her reclusion was certainly a sort of miracle that no sectary could ever imitate. That alone might suffice to enlighten well-formed minds, by teaching them the infallibility of the Catholic Church, since no other, could boast of a member endowed with that magnanimous strength and heroic constancy, which our heroine always displayed.

CHAPTER VI.

Sister Le Ber's constitution being weak, her austerities should have caused her to endure acute sufferings, for she practised the most abject poverty in her clothing and apartment and although her food was very coarse and common, she did not partake of any delicacies, even, on the greatest feasts. As love towards Jesus in the Blessed Sacrament had led her to choose this austere life, it also induced her to adopt other mortifications ; thus, deeming her usual food too choice, she often set it aside, to fast on bread and water, or else, she took so very little soup or boiled meat, that many were astonished how she could live. Mother Juchereau adds, that sister Le Ber often took food, which she had kept until it had become quite mouldy.

Her linen was very coarse, she frequently wore but woollen garments, which she mended repeatedly before laying them aside ; and we previously mentioned that she always wore a hair

shirt, or a belt of the same material. She suf-
fered from cold during the greater part of the year;
for, although her room contained that indispensable
piece of Canadian furniture, a stove, she seldom
heated it sufficiently to protect her from the inclemency of the weather; summer in no wise, mitigated
her sufferings, for the high temperature of her
apartment was sometimes suffocating: yet, she
never drew near the window to enjoy the cool
breeze which arose at certain hours. Such were
some of the effects produced by her ardent love for
the Heavenly Guest, who dwelt in the Tabernacle.

She found additional means of mortifying herself in the practice of her rule of life, which she
followed most assiduously. During her residence
of twenty years in the Convent of the Congregation de Notre-Dame, from Easter to All Saint's
day, she arose at 4 o'clock; $4\frac{1}{2}$ was her hour of rising
during the remainder of the year. She then de-
voted one hour to her first meditation, recited part
of the office of the Blessed Virgin, assisted at
the Holy Sacrifice of the Mass, during a certain
part of which she remained with outstretched
arms. She read some spiritual work, from nine till
half past nine and meditated from ten to eleven;
she then read a chapter of the New Testament and
made her particular examination. She dined at
$11\frac{1}{2}$; recited the Vespers and Complin of the
Little Office at one, and at four devoted another
hour to mental prayer. She supped at six, recited
the rosary and other vocal prayers at seven; and

retired at half past eight. But on Sundays and holidays she devoted two other hours to meditation, one during High Mass, and the other during Vespers. We have already alluded to her habit of rising every night to meditate; then, she recited Matin and Lauds; on the eve of feasts this mental prayer lasted two hours, though on the following day, five hours were devoted to the same exercise.

Such was the division of her time, between work, spiritual reading and exercises of piety; we shall here enter into some details concerning her various occupations.

As sister Le Ber had always carefully avoided idleness, she never took any recreation; needle work occupied her during the hours which intervened between her religious exercises. Jesus Christ was the sole end of all her actions, so that when she worked, she sought to relieve His suffering members, or to honor Himself in the Blessed Sacrament by decorating His sanctuary, or by making vestments for His ministers. She sometimes spun and knitted, both for the poor and for herself, but always gave them the best, appropriating the most inferior articles for her own use; her stockings, for instance, were made of the coarsest wool or a species of twine which the poorest classes would not have used. Her tender love for Christ's suffering members, prompted her to bestow large alms on them and to deprive herself of many necessaries. Respect for the Blessed Sacrament, her constant Guest, and a desire of assisting the poor to her utmost capacity, led her to sew pieces of old leather on the soles of her husk shoes, to make them last longer, and to prevent any noise being heard in the sanctuary, when she moved about her apartment.

Making altar linen and church ornaments was her principal occupation; she excelled in embroidery, all admired her work; she blended gold, silk, silver and wool, with wonderful taste and ingenuity; and imparted such beauty and natural to all her embroidery, that it was considered as a model. She had never learned drawing; yet displayed considerable taste and regularity in tracing the patterns which she composed. It would be no easy task to enumerate all the different specimens of work produced by her industry, for she was both active and ingenious. Mr. de Belmont's statement confirms this opinion of her industry. In 1721 he wrote, saying: Her benevo- " lence was not limited to the Nuns of the " Congregation de Notre-Dame, on whom she " bestowed many gifts for the church; the Northern " and Southern parishes of the district of Mon- " treal possess many specimens of her work, such " as altar fronts, flowers and vestments." A set of vestments which she made, may be seen at the Parish Church of Ville-Marie; they are embroidered on a silver ground, and are such striking proofs of her devotion, that they should be care fully kept with the treasures of the Church.

She sanctified the hours allotted to work by reflecting on what she had read. The Psalter and the New-Testament were her favourite books ; for as the Psalter contains the interior dispositions of Jesus Christ, faithful souls find therein means of imitating their Heavenly Spouse. The New-Testament teaches them the path to perfection and points out the goal of all their desires, by relating the soul-strenghtening words and benevolent actions of their Divine Master. Sister Le Ber had read both these books so frequently, that she could recite the greater part of them from memory.

Spiritual reading was however only one of her many exercises of piety, for she had adopted several practises of devotion and recited a large number of vocal prayers. Besides those for morning and evening, she daily recited the Office of the Cross, the Litany of the Saints, the Little Office and the Rosary ; she said the office of the Dead three times a week, that the colony might be protected by the souls of so many fervent Christians whom the Iroquois had murdered. Ville-Marie having often been reduced to the last extremity and the most atrocious cruelties having been perpetrated against the colonists, they lived in continual dread of the Dutch, English, and Iroquois whom they regarded as their common enemies. In 1691 this induced the citizens, particularly Mr. James Le Ber, to adopt means of obtaining the protection of the souls who had been liberated from Purgatory, and particularly those of their fellow citizens who had died in defending their country. For this purpose they bound themselves by vow to have a funeral service celebrated for these souls, every week during a year; and to erect a chapel near the Parish Church where masses for the dead might always be offered. As sister Le Ber was a victim immolated to God to draw down His blessings on her country, she took part in this public devotion and adhered to it after the year had expired. Hence, notwithstanding all her other prayers, she recited the office for the Dead three times a week.

These numerous prayers and the exercises of piety, practised by one who, during so many years, led such a severe and penitential life, are striking proofs of sister Le Ber's heroic virtue, and of the ardent love she bore Jesus Christ, whom she worshipped in the Sacrament of His love. Still she experienced no consolation while she led this austere life; no human aid came forward to strengthen her fortitude when nature was weary of continued efforts; neither did she receive from above those consolations generally experienced by the faithful spouses of the Lord. This fact certainly imparted additional merit to her virtue; and displayed the strength, magnanimity and constancy with which she was endowed.

CHAPTER VII.

MISS LE BER PERSEVERES IN ALL HER RELI-
GIOUS EXERCISES. NOTWITHSTANDING HER
SEVERAL TRIALS, SHE OBEYS HER DIRECTOR
AND SEEKS CONSOLATION FROM GOD ALONE.

The fact that sister Le Ber daily devoted four
hours to meditation, and on some days five and
seven, may have led our readers to believe that this
exercise was most agreeable to her, and that she
found therein all sorts of spiritual delights and heavenly comforts; such however was not the case,
although God had been pleased to draw her
to Himself, by bestowing great consolations
when she first embraced a retired life; He withdrew them before she entered the Congregation, and from this moment until her death,
she was tried in so severe a manner, that those
only who have passed through the same ordeal, can
conceive and understand it.

This is the path allotted to peculiarly holy
souls, and those are the means generally used by
the Almighty to enable them to attain the pinnacle

of spiritual perfection. These celestial delights which God first bestows on souls to draw them lovingly to Himself, do not inculcate virtue, but merely impart a love of it, for virtue is the prize awarded to labour and suffering. God uses these consolations, as mothers do delicacies, to induce children to fulfil their duty : so long as these rewards are required, it is evident that love of duty is not deeply rooted in those children's hearts. Thus, when a soul experiences consolations which no wise tend to elevate it, it is evidently feeble and but little advanced in virtue.

God was pleased to treat sister Le Ber, as He does heroic souls; and to teach her solid virtue which is founded on interior abnegation. He deprived her of the celestial light which had illumined her soul for many years, and withdrew those ineffable consolations which had previously drawn her towards Him, and had often seemed to give her wings to reach the throne of God. This must not lead us to think that Our Kind Father forsakes those whom He tries in this manner, He acts thus, to enable them to attain perfection, for in withdrawing those particular sensible graces which do not influence the soul's superior faculties, He endows the latter with more lasting and more estimable gifts. When the Almighty withdrew these favours from sister Le Ber, her hours of meditation became hours of severe trial : her mind seemed darkened, and her heart cold and callous. Faith in the wisdom of God's decrees was her sole guide;

and His holy will, her only consolation.   True it
is, that the Almighty sometimes rewarded His servant's fidelity, by enlightening her mind with a ray
of celestial light from above, and comforting her soul
by pouring on it one drop of those ineffable consolations which He alone can bestow; but then the
darkness grew darker still, and the heart's usual aridity would return.   Thus it was she spent the last
twenty years of her life ; and these trials tended to
strengthen her virtue. Her fidelity throughout this
long ordeal ought to teach souls how steadfast they
should remain, when God is pleased to test their
virtue. Many get discouraged when they experience
this apparent aridity, and forsake their exercises
because they have lost the inclination which attracted them.   Our holy Recluse acted not thus ;
she persevered as faithfully in fulfilling her exercises
of piety during her twenty years of trial, as she
had done when enjoying all sorts of spiritual comforts : she never omitted nor abridged any of her
long meditations, and eagerly rose at night to devote
a considerable time to mental prayer, although she
acquitted herself of this duty without experiencing
any sensible devotion. She was scrupulously faithful in performing her various duties at the time
appointed for each. This struck Anna Barroy
her cousin and attendant ; she was not aware
of sister Le Ber's interior trials, but could not help
remarking her inalterable fidelity to her rule of life.
She subsequently became a Nun of the Congregation de Notre-Dame, and was obliged to write an

account of sister Le Ber. Our heroine's punctuality to her rule chiefly elicited her admiration: " Sister Le Ber complied so exactly with all " her rule required, that she can be looked upon " as a model of punctuality, and as an encourage- " ment to the most fervent to renew their zeal in " following all their rules, even the most trifling " points; her example also condemns slightest " omissions." Fidelity to these regulations, through a pure motive of love for God, was consequently, one of the results of sisterLe Ber's trials.

When God sanctifies souls by trial, if they persevere in their exercises of piety, other temptations assail them: the enemy of all good endeavours to lead them astray by convincing them that this state of spiritual dryness injures the soul; and that they must make some effort to free themselves from it. The better to ensure success in his evil designs, he tries to persuade them that their director does not understand the trials under which they labour, or, that he has not sufficient grace to guide them: he tempts them to seek another spiritual director, and deludes them by the hope of thus advancing in virtue. Many yield to the temptation, and leave their confessor without asking advice, and without any reasons to authorize their doing so; they do not reflect that a sincere desire of ensuring their salvation is not their motive; but that they are actuated by a hope that this change will prove beneficial by obtaining consolation.

But Sister Le Ber was not blinded by self-love, she warded off all its attacks, hence she never would consent to change her director, nor would she even agree to consult any one else.   Seeing that she experienced no consolation in obeying him, he repeatedly advised her to choose some more enlightened person, who might encourage her in the hours of trial : she refused to do so ; although she might have had recourse to distinguished members of the society of Jesus, or to some of the Recollet Friars then residing in Ville-Marie, or even to another priest of the Seminary of Saint-Sulpice : she adhered to her director, thinking as he had been the instrument of enlightening her childhood and of guiding her first steps in the path to perfection, she would walk in safety so long as she followed his advice.   Nought but a most lively Faith could have inspired such perseverance and have taught her to view her confessor, as the guide whom God had chosen to direct her through life ; for although Mr. Séguenot was parish priest at Pointe-aux-Trembles during twenty years, she never made choice of another director during his life.   While he had charge of this parish, he seldom came to Ville-Marie more than once a week, and then he heard Miss Le Ber's confession. His absence, the impossibility of consulting him in unexpected circumstances and the difficulties of seeing, him when the roads were bad, might have sanctioned a change of director, yet she never would have any other.   Her submission

to him was such that some time before her death,
Mr. Séguenot being too unwell to administer the
Sacrament during the night, she would not receive
Holy Communion without her director's permission
although another priest offered to replace him.

Another temptation assails those who are afflicted by interior trials : not experiencing any consolation in fulfilling their religious duties, they seek
it in creatures and indulge in conversations on
pious subjects, hoping thereby to alleviate their sufferings or at least to forget them for a time ; sister
Le Ber however never yielded to these insinuations of the evil spirit ; in the midst of her severe
trials, she never deviated from the resolution she
had taken on retiring from the world, that of seek.
ing consolation from God alone.   Being at liberty
to modify her rule of life, she might have requested
her superiors to grant her some objects of amusement, or to converse with fervent souls on topics
which might have tended to strengthen her virtue,
and induce her to persevere ; yet, far from soliciting any such favour, she refused it when offered.

She always endeavoured to imitate Saint John
the Baptist, who, during his long retreat deprived himself of all intercourse with creatures,
and of all the comforts of life.   The better to en.
sure her perseverance, she frequently called to mind
what is said of Saint John : " As he lived in the
" hope of beholding the Saviour of the world, he
" never looked on created objects with any satis-
" faction."   Hence sister Le Ber declined all offers

she received, and would not consent to have a small garden near her cell, where she could breathe the fresh air and take some little relaxation. On one occasion, she happened to be ill, and her confessor proposed that she should leave her apartment for change of air : she refused saying : " O " Father, my cell is my terrestrial paradise ; it is " my centre of attraction. Can a fish live out of " water ? I could find no more pleasant or saluta- " ry dwelling, no palace could render me as happy " as my cell does ; it is dearer to me than the " entire universe."

We shall hereafter relate how earnestly she entreated the Nuns of the Congregation to erect a new building for their schools. As this wing was erected at her request, and as she defrayed part of the expense, the Nun who directed its construction, obtained permission to speak to sister Le Ber, and asked if she would come to visit the building, when it would be finished. Our holy Recluse had never seen the plan, nor did she know on what precise spot the building was erected, although she daily heard the men working at it, and might have seen it without going any considerable distance from her cell ; she answered with her usual mildness : " I do not think that my presence would be neces- " sary, but I shall see about it."

The Nun understood her desire and said no more on this subject. Her love of mortification prompted her to conquer nature to such a degree that she never looked out into the Convent garden which surrounded her retirement, nor did she ever cast a glance on her father's garden situated but a few paces from her cell.

She also deprived herself of all consolation that was not absolutely necessary, or ordered by her director. On entering her cell in the Convent of the Congregation de Notre-Dame, Mr. Seguenot had stipulated that should his Lordship the Bishop of Quebec express a desire of seeing her, she must acquiesce to it, and that Mr. Le Ber her father could visit her twice a year; she observed this point most scrupulously, never asking to see her father more frequently. Mr. Le Ber lavished the deepest affection on his only daughter whose innocence and eminent virtues had won his confidence and veneration. His fond parental love led him to request the favour of being buried in the church of the Congregation, so that death might bring him nearer to his daughter, and that their remains one day might rest in the same spot. Sister Le Ber was truly attached to her father, for gratitude and religion had strengthened natural fondness; yet she never asked to quit her cell in order to console him when he lay on his death-bed : she testified her love by praying for him. His death inflicted a deep wound on her affectionate heart. Her father's funeral service was celebrated in the church adjoining her cell. Though she did not behold the scene of mourning, she must needs have heard the sorrowful chants that accompany such ceremonies. Her conduct throughout deserves the highest ap-

K

plause, for notwithstanding the anguish she experienced on that day, she fulfilled all her usual
duties.

She was really fond of her other relatives and
acted very generously towards some who were not
in affluent circumstances, devoting considerable
sums to the education of some of her little cousins,
who would otherwise have been brought up in ignorance. But this affection for her relatives did not
lead her to transgress her rule of silence. After
her reclusion she refused to receive visits from any
of them : she would not even consent to see her
nephews de Saint Paul and de Senneville who were
not acquainted with her. The only means to catch
a glimpse of her was to kneel near the sanctuary
when she received Holy Communion. A praiseworthy curiosity induced several persons to assist
at Mass on those days ; they were amply rewarded ;
for her profound religion and unassuming modesty
produced salutary impressions.

Besides the Bishop and Mr. Le Ber, the Superioress of the Congregation was the only person
who visited the holy Recluse, her visits were limited to one or two during the year; for the rule
which sister Le Ber had adopted with her director's sanction, forbade all unnecessary communication ; hence necessity alone sometimes led her to
speak to her attendant. If she required a Nun to
attend her when sick, she merely asked what she
required; when well she left a note upon the
window containing a list of what she wanted, she

never opened any notes found there, before sending them to her director.

Nevertheless a special favour was occasionally granted to some of the Nuns of the Congregation; they were allowed to consult her in difficulties and interior trials; for during all the time she underwent that ordeal of which we previously spoke, she lost none of her natural gentleness and always expressed her thoughts with great facility. These trials purified her, as fire does gold, and endowed her with a personal knowledge of the difficulties encountered in a spiritual life. She was thus enabled to direct souls in the midst of interior darkness. Her religious love of silence and her fidelity to this point of her rule had drawn down on her words the power of touching souls and of imbuing them with her own fervour. She spoke so feelingly, and God's Holy Spirit so blessed her language, that all who conversed with her, withdrew filled with holy dispositions, and determined to bear every trial through love for God and to promote His glory.

She lost all control over herself when allowed to speak on religious subjects; this happened whenever she conversed with her director; but Mother Juchereau informs us that she seldom indulged in lengthened intercourse even with him. Mr. de Belmont says: " Her fervour overpowered her completely; she spoke with such feeling and rapidity that her confessor was frequently obliged to moderate her zeal. She would then cast herself on her knees saying: Father, forgive me ; you are right in warning me of my indiscretion. She would remain in this humble posture without uttering a word until her confessor gave her permission to speak.   Then her usual eloquence would return, and she would pour forth those Evangelical truths which were so indelibly imprinted on her heart. The intensity of feeling, facility of expressing her thoughts and the irresistible ardour, which sister Le Ber manifested, when speaking of God, were evident proofs that her trials contributed to teach her the ways of Divine Love, and the path to that solid perfection which is founded on self-abnegation.   None can help admiring her fidelity to silence in the midst of such severe trials, and this fidility may be truly termed heroic, when we reflect that it was practised unremittingly during thirty-four years.

BOOK FOURTH.

SISTER LE BER'S DEVOTION TO THE BLESSED
VIRGIN.—HER AFFECTION FOR THE CON-
GREGATION DE NOTRE DAME.—HER HOLY
DEATH.

CHAPTER I.

SISTER LE BER'S FILIAL DEVOTION TO THE BLESSED VIRGIN.

Jesus Christ truly present in the Adorable Sacrament of the altar, was the object of Sister Le
Ber's special devotion, and to prove her love for,
and faith in the Divine Presence, she deprived herself of all earthly comforts, dwelt in poverty and
solitude, devoted many hours to mental prayer,
worked assiduously, gave up all intercourse with
the creature, and accomplished those other heroic
acts, which previously elicited our admiration.
Jesus in the Holy Eucharist was then the centre of

all her devotions, the sole object of her love ; and, to approach nearer, to the beloved of her heart, she united her intentions to the interior dispositions of that spotless Virgin, who is Jesus Christ's most perfect worshipper.

Enlightened by Divine Faith, she felt that she enjoyed the happiness of being the temple of the Holy Ghost. Knowing that this Holy Spirit is the source of the spiritual life which is bestowed on all Saints, she endeavoured to conform her inclinations to those which He had created within Mary's soul. To ensure fidelity to this practice, she frequently meditated on an engraving representing Mary's interior life,—The Blessed Virgin is seen surrounded by clouds ; the Holy Ghost in the form of a bright dove, rests on her bosom, indicating that the abundance of His gifts, was bestowed upon her ; her eyes are fixed on the monogram. "*Jesus Saviour of Mankind.*" This engraving signified, that as the Holy Ghost was the principle of all Mary's actions ; the love of Jesus, and the salvation of souls constituted her sole aim ; beneath was written an invitation to unite in these interior dispositions; *with Mary, through Mary, and in Mary.*

This holy union was Sister Le Ber's chief study during her years of solitude:—her meditations, the Holy Sacrifice of the Mass, her Communions, and other acts of devotion, her manual labor, even her meals and minor occupations, were, by Faith and Love, united to Mary's interior dispositions.

She was wont to beg of this Holy Virgin, to be ever with her, to be the model of her actions, the soul of her soul; to imbue her, so completely, with her own Holy dispositions, that she might consider herself an instrument her Heavenly Mother could use, as she pleased, to contribute to Jesus' glory. To be more thoroughly penetrated with feelings of this entire trust in Mary, Sister Le Ber had another picture, which represented the Blessed Virgin receiving the soul of a Christian, who seemed to pine, at the protracted length, of her exile; and, to place all her happiness, in resting entirely on Mary; written below this engraving, was a touching invocation, which Sister Le Ber daily said with love and confidence. . Devotion to Mary's interior life, and a desire of imitating it, were the means our heroine sought to become agreeable to Jesus; wishing to copy Mary in all things, she adopted a woollen garment, of a whitish grey color; but her peculiar study, was the *Interior life*, for she well knew, that it alone had induced the Holy Trinity, to shower the choicest blessings on this humble Virgin.   Hence, every year she followed the custom of the Ecclesiastics of the Seminary of Ville Marie, who celebrated, on the 19th of October, a feast, in honor of the *Interior of Mary*.   In preparation for this festival, she fasted the previous day, on bread and water.   Mary's interior life being the chief object of her devotion towards the Blessed Virgin, and neglecting however, none of Her other mysteries, she left a memorial still existing of it, in the chasuble she embroidered for the Parish Church. Knowing that this vestment would be used on festivals of the Blessed Virgin, she embroidered a medallion in the centre, representing Mary's interior life, similar to the engraving she had in her cell; for she desired that the faithful should know this devotion, which experience had taught her to cherish, because of the many blessings and consolations attending it. Sister Le Ber during her conversation with her attendant, frequently told her, that her fondest desire was to honor and imitate Mary, and to induce others to act in like manner. We feel confident that her devoted love for the Mother of Jesus must have drawn down this Immaculate Virgin's protection on the colony. The little care that had been taken at our heroine's death to collect memoirs of her life, has doubtlessly deprived us of several edifying traits; one however has been handed to us, and proves the happy results of her confidence in Mary's powerful intercession. The English had long sought to conquer Canada, and in 1711 formed plans to carry out their designs. 3000 men, left New York with small field pieces to surprise Ville Marie by land; whilst a fleet was sent out to attack Quebec. Each of these armies was more numerous, than the united forces of Canada; Ville Marie's sole fortification being a pike fence, it could not resist the attack, and the citizens were in despair. While consternation thus reigned, Ann Barroy was told to inform Sister Le Ber of the coming calamity, that her prayers might protect her fellow countrymen; when the Holy Recluse heard the above mentioned details, she remained silent for some time, then consoled her attendant, assuring her that the Blessed Virgin would guard the country. As news was received that the land army had left New York, the citizens expected to see the city besieged by the enemy. Sister Le Ber gave her cousin a picture of the Blessed Virgin, on which she had written a prayer, beseeching this Holy Mother, to watch over the Congregation. She told her cousin to fasten this picture on the barn door; the prayer was as follows:

" Queen of Angels, our sovereign and bountiful " Mother, your daughters of the Congregation con- " fide in you, their sole confidence is in your power- " ful intercession; relying on your benevolence, " they hope that you will not allow your enemies " to take possession of that which belongs to those " who are under your special protection."

As soon as the picture was fastened to the door, several individuals hastened to the Congregation requesting Sister Le Ber to write prayers on pictures, which they brought for the purpose; for all considered her a saint; as her humility prevented her from acquiescing in their request, some of them being dissatisfied took possession of the original picture, and she was obliged to write the same prayer on another. This confidence in Sister Le Ber's prayers was not limited to the lower classes; the following instance proves that the most distinguished persons held her in the highest esteem.

The Baron of Longueuil, our heroine's cousin, justly surnamed the *Machabeus* of Montreal, happened to be Governor of Ville Marie, when the English threatened Canada; he thought that the enemy should not be allowed to reach the city without being attacked; and the safest plan would be to lie in ambush at some distance from the city; consequently, he determined to set out with a handful of men to surprise the English near Chambly, where they had to pass; but, as his whole reliance was in the protection of that Holy Mother who had been chosen Sovereign of the country, he wished to march with a banner, having the Blessed Virgin on one side, and on the other a prayer, written, and composed by Sister Le Ber. Our heroine could not refuse this request; made the banner, and placed on it a picture of the Immaculate Virgin, which her brother had painted some time previous, and wrote this prayer on the canvass; " *Our enemies rely on the power of their* " *arms, and we on the powerful intercession of Her* " *whom we revere and invoke as Queen of Angels.* " *She is terrible as an army set in array, with Her* " *assistance we will vanquish our enemies.*" Mr. de Belmont, the Superior of the Seminary, blessed the banner, and solemnly gave it to the Baron, in presence of a large number of the faithful, who had assembled in the Parish Church, to witness this edifying scene. The brave and valiant captain hastened to depart, carrying with him a banner which he considered as a token of protection from above.

When Sister Le Ber's cousin informed her of
the coming calamity, she added; " If the English
" have a favourable wind, their fleet will be before
" Quebec on such a day, and the fate of the colony
" will be sealed."—Our holy Recluse after remaining silent for some time reassured her cousin, saying :—" Sister, your fears will not be realized,
the Blessed Virgin will watch over this country;
She is our Guardian should we apprehend any
danger ?

She thus formally declared that Mary's powerful
intercession would prevent the English from having
the favourable wind they desired; for their number
led them to suppose that, by an unexpected attack,
they could easily master the French colonists.

This prophetic answer induces us to believe that
Sister Le Ber had subsequently offered up many
prayers to the Blessed Virgin, to obtain that the
enemy's progress might be arrested; this was undoubtedly the object of her long meditations, both
night and day; for she was aware that her fellow-
citizens were in a state of fearful apprehension.
Worldly wisdom would doubtlessly condemn the
calm assurance with which Sister Le Ber quieted
her cousin's fears; but time proved that her reply
had been inspired from above; and what Geneviève
had been to old France, so Jeanne Le Ber was to
be to New France, our heroine's prayers were to be
the means of warding off the impending ruin of the
colony; for after the English fleet, destined to
attack Quebec, had entered the St. Lawrence and

lay to the North of Isle aux Œufs, a violent south
wind arose and seven of the largest ships were
dashed to pieces on the rocks. Thunder and light-
ning tended to render the scene still more terrific;
one ship was struck so violently that its keel was
thrown far up on land.

About three thousand corpses were found on the
banks; two entire companies of the Queen's guards
were identified by their uniform.

This disaster so intimidated the English admi-
ral, that apprehending the loss of the remainder
of his fleet, he returned directly to London with a
few ships. Not wishing to appear before the Queen
after this defeat, he set fire to his ships on entering the Thames; two sailors were the only persons
who escaped; the land forces which had been sent
to attack Ville Marie returned on hearing that the
fleet had been destroyed. The general consternation occasioned by the misfortunes of the English,
was increased in Boston the day of their return;
eighty houses having been destroyed by fire.

The Canadians considered this event as a striking proof of the special protection granted to their
country. Mr. de Vaudreuil, Governor General of
Canada, wrote to the Minister of the French Navy,
saying:

" We will return thanks to God for the mira-
" culous protection He has been pleased to bestow
" on this colony. All agree in saying, that the
" Almighty has conferred a great blessing on the
" colonists, by destroying the English fleet, with-
" out any loss on our side."

CHAPTER II.

SISTER LE BER'S DEVOTION TO THE BLESSED
VIRGIN MARY, INSPIRES HER WITH A RE-
LIGIOUS VENERATION FOR SISTER BOUR-
GEOYS AND A SPECIAL AFFECTION FOR THE
CONGREGATION.

Respect, confidence and filial love for the Blessed
Virgin were the links that united Sister Le Ber to the
venerable Sister Bourgeoys, whom she considered,
as a living representative of this heavenly Mother.
During her conversations with her cousin, Ann
Barroy, when the latter was about to enter Sister
Bourgeoy's Institution, she frequently said to her,
that the odour of this holy Foundress' virtue had
drawn her thither, that she had come after a great
many other holy souls, whose fervor she held in high
veneration, to enclose herself in their blessed solitude. She never wearied extolling Sister Bourgeoys' merits; and when she gave any advice to
the Sisters of the Congregation, respecting their
rule of life, she always held forth their Foundress
as a perfect model of all that the Church required
of a true Sister of the Congregation. These praises
may certainly be considered as the greatest eulo-

gium that Sister Bourgeoys could receive, for our
holy Recluse had attained that high degree of wisdom and penetration into divine matters, that God
alone can give.

This veneration was reciprocal, Sister Bourgeoys
viewed Miss Le Ber with feelings of the most profound respect, on account of the sublime virtues
she had so often admired in her. Although these
favoured souls dwelt beneath the same roof, they
seldom had any intercourse, yet both seemed to
delight in praising each other's merits; this mutual religious veneration was inspired by a super-
natural light, which enabled the one to discern the
many virtues that adorned the other's soul. Hence,
if Sister Le Ber experienced feelings of delight on
entering her cell in the Convent of the Congregation, Sister Bourgeoys hailed her arrival there
with no less joy and gratitude. Several years later
she spoke of it, in the following terms : " I was
" delighted when Miss Le Ber entered this institu-
" tion to imitate Magdalen's retirement in a grot-
" to, by dwelling in a cell. She never quits
" this abode nor speaks to any one; her food is
" conveyed to her by a door outside of the chapel
" and she receives it through a small aperture. A
" small grating enables her to look at the taberna-
" cle and to receive Holy Communion."

Personal esteem for our holy Recluse and for
her eminent qualities was not the sole motive of
Sister Bourgeoys' satisfaction ; our heroine's mode
of life during her stay in the Congregation also

elicited the venerable Foundress' heartfelt gratitude towards the Sovereign Author of all good.   A
pious thought had once been expressed to Sister
Bourgeoys by her director, previous to her coming
to Canada. Our Lord, said he, after His ascension into Heaven, left three classes of women to
follow and work for His Church.   Some, called to
the exercise of a contemplative life, are represented
by St. Mary Magdalen ; others, whose vocation
lead them to the cloister, there to devote their lives,
to their neighbour's welfare, have St. Martha for
a model ; but, how many of a third kind, have been
called to imitate the active life of the Blessed Virgin
who contributed, so largely, to the sanctification of
souls, and that, outside the limits of a cloister : such
was to be the end of the order Sister Bourgeoys
was one day to form, and has been fully realized
in the Institution of the Congregation de Notre
Dame at Ville Marie.

It is to be remembered that when Miss Le Ber
withdrew to the Congregation in 1695, the Hospital Nuns happened to be there; their Convent
having been lately destroyed by fire.   Seeing these
persons united, Sister Bourgeoys called to mind
the reflection which her Director had made to her,
when she was very young; this circumstance,
tended to heighten her delight, on receiving our
heroine : the following are her impressions on this
coincidence.   " Since Miss Le Ber has entered
" this Institution to dwell in retirement I have
" beheld the three classes of women, whom our

" Lord left to minister to the wants of His Church ;
" the first, leading a solitary life, like St. Magda-
" len ; the second by imitating Martha's activity ;
" and the third, endeavouring to reproduce the
" Blessed Virgin's zeal for the salvation of souls.
" These three orders are now united beneath one
" roof : Miss Le Ber having been called to re-
" present Magdalen, who dwelt in the grotto, as
" St. John the Baptist had dwelt in the wilderness.
" The Hospital Nuns have been here for some
" time, and remind us of Martha's busy, though
" cloistered life. The Nuns of the Congregation
" de Notre Dame, represent the Blessed Virgin,
" their Mother, Superioress, and Foundress. She
" alone embraces all the different callings of the
" Church, and protects all religious orders. This
" Holy Mother is pleased, then, to unite these
" three classes of women within Her house, to teach
" us, that a bond of universal charity, should unite
" us to those, who are devoted to God's service, under
" Her Holy protection."

Sister Le Ber's special attachment to the Congregation, arose from the belief, that this community was Mary's cherished family; and this led
her to bestow benefits upon it; hence, after defray-
ing a great part of the expense incurred by building the new Church, and richly decorating it ; she
also founded the Perpetual Adoration, and bestowed
a large sum to enable the Nuns to have the Holy
Sacrifice of the Mass, daily offered up in their chapel. Wishing to uphold a Community so dear to

her, and so favoured by the Queen of Angels, she left them a gift of 10,000 livres; saying, in the contract, that " *affection for the Nuns of the Con-* " *gregation de Notre Dame induced her to present* " *this offering.*" She stipulated, that the revenue of this sum should always be used for the maintenance of the Community at Ville Marie, and for no other purpose.

Mr. Le Ber had also during his life time, evinced great respect for this institution, and before death gave a striking proof of his affection.

Although the Sisters of the Congregation exacted no dower when candidates had none, he bequeathed 2,000 livres to the Nuns, for the purpose of admitting Ann Barroy, should she be called to a religious life; or any other person whom Sister Le Ber and the Nuns might select. He also left a legacy of 3,000 livres as a dower for one of his nieces, Mary Elizabeth Lemoyne de Longueuil, if she wished to enter the Congregation.* Ann Barroy

---

* This generosity from Mr. Le Ber is a striking proof of his refined and delicate feelings; his daughter having already bestowed many gifts on the Congregation, he might have requested the Nuns to admit Ann Barroy without any dower; or to act towards her, as they did towards some others; to receive her gratuitously, merely stipulating that she might inherit something later. But Mr. Le Ber wished to act in a fatherly manner, and left her the dower which wealthy parents generally gave their daughters. Many parents have frequently adopted a different line of conduct; some, though in affluent circumstances, have alleged different reasons for de-

had dwelt in the Congregation de Notre Dame ever since Sister Le Ber had entered her cell; she had been most favourably impressed with the fervour which reigned among the Sisters; and God was pleased to call her to enter this institution. She had probably informed her cousin of this fact, previous to Mr. Le Ber's death, for it appears that his daughter requested him to assign the above sum to the Nuns. This opinion is confirmed by Ann Barroy who thus mentioned Sister Le Ber's pleasure when she spoke of entering the Congregation. She said, " I never experienced more heart- " felt satisfaction than I did, when you expressed " your desire of becoming a member of this Com-

---

priving their daughters of their rights, and have thus injured the Community that was bound to support their children.

In 1718, Mary Chapt de Lacorne, entered the Convent of the Congregation; she was called Sister of the Blessed Sacrament, and spent forty years in this institution, without receiving any dower: on her entry, her father said his numerous family prevented him from settling any fixed sum on her; but that, at his death she would inherit her share of his fortune. Some years after this Nun's death, her eldest brother was shipwreck,ed on board the " Auguste," and the Community claimed the portion which had rightly belonged to her. Another brother Mr. St. Luc de Lacorne, refused to grant the slightest compensation to the Nuns of the Congregation saying that they possessed no will, or written contract in their favour. As this occurred after the conquest of Canada by the British, the matter was referred to the court of the Captains of Militia, and the Lacorne family

" munity, and I will most willingly defray all the
" expenses, this step may incur."

Sister Le Ber's delight on receiving this intelligence arose, not only from a natural feeling of
pleasure at the thought, that a member of her
family was about to consecrate herself to God;
but also, from the fact that her cousin had selected
an institution so specially consecrated to the Blessed
Virgin ; an institution wherein she was honoured
as Foundress, Superioress, Queen, and Mother.

The mere appellation " *Congregation de Notre
Dame*" made a deep impression on Sister Le Ber ;
it had attached her to the institution from childhood, and had induced her to select it as her abode.
Her marked predilection for the Nuns, sprung from
a belief, that God had chosen them, to represent

---

was condemned. The principal members appealed to
Sir Thomas Gage, Governor of Montreal ; he took the
matter into consideration and finally confirmed the con-
demnation of the Lacorne family, by sentencing them to
give two thousand livres to the Sisters of the Congregation as the deceased Nun's dower, and to pay the interest of that sum from 1718 ; he settled the entire
amount at 2,750 livres ; and allowed the family to give
the sum to the Sisters ; or to give them the inheritance of the eldest Lacorne, which would have rightly
belonged to his Sister, if she had lived.—The Governor
being a Protestant, could not be accused of partiality
towards religious Institutions; but a sense of justice,
led him to acknowledge the rights of the Sisters of the
Congregation; and although the Lacorne family were
Catholics, he showed them the importance of this obligation, and reproved them for neglecting to fulfil it.—

the Blessed Virgin, and to edify the faithful, by endeavouring to imitate Her Apostolic zeal, and other eminent virtues. Hence, after Ann Barroy's reception, now Sister St. Charles, our Holy Recluse often said to her : " What happiness you enjoy to " be thus numbered among Mary's daughters ! Do " you fully appreciate this favour ? Are you tho- " roughly instructed in all that your state requires " of you ? Do you practise entire separation from " the world, and from all natural inclinations ? She, " who wears the Blessed Virgin's livery, should be " detached from all worldly things ; she should " avoid affectation of manners, extreme neatness, " and all that tends to singularity."

Sister St. Charles once entered her cousin's cell with a coarse dress, that had not yet lost its lustre ; Sister Le Ber remarked it, and advised her to wear it in the rain ; the religious adds: " On another occasion, I had a dress so very old and worn, that I feared her displeasure ; being fully aware, how much she disliked extremes, knowing they gene- rally proceed from a desire of singularity rather than from solid virtue ; but she was delighted, on seeing my dress, and took advantage of it, to extol the virtue of poverty ; a virtue, she added, so cherished by our Holy Mother the Blessed Virgin; her words were so convincing and per- suasive, that on withdrawing from her cell, I resolved to practise it more faithfully than I had hitherto done."

Sister Le Ber's esteem for the Sisters of the

Congregation, and her appreciation of the manifold benefits they conferred on the colony, by educating youth, induced her to bestow another gift, which enabled them to enlarge their Schools.

CHAPTER III. .

RESPECT FOR SISTER BOURGEOYS, INDUCES MISS
LE BER TO ENABLE THE NUNS OF THE
CONGREGATION DE NOTRE DAME TO BUILD
A BOARDING SCHOOL; SHE SETTLES A DONA-
TION FOR THE GRATUITOUS EDUCATION OF
A NUMBER OF BOARDERS.

When Sister Bourgeoys laid the foundations of
the building of the Congregation, she little thought
that the community would increase so rapidly; but
she soon perceived that her buildings were not
sufficiently extensive to accommodate the Nuns,
and pupils; so before her death, she advised the
Nuns to erect new buildings for the different
schools of the city. The Holy Foundress died
in 1700, and the Nuns were unable to carry out
this design; their funds being very low, owing
to the expenses incurred by establishing several
missions, and the scarcity caused by protracted
wars.

Miss Le Ber intended after her father's
death, to divest herself of all her inheritance in
favour of the Nuns of the Congregation de Notre

Dame, to enable them to extend the sphere of their duties, with less difficulty than they had previously encountered: she had also a strong desire of realizing her revered friend's dying request, and wished not only to supply funds for building large schools; but also, to settle a donation for the education of children, whose parents had not the means of so doing. Fear, lest her funds would not meet the expense, caused her to defer; but a presentiment that death was near induced her to hasten the accomplishment of her generous resolution. After soliciting Mary's protection and that of the Holy Angels, she settled a sum for the gratuitous education of a certain number of young girls, but not being able to defray the expense of the building, she earnestly requested the Sisters to rely on Providence, and to begin the undertaking without any further delay.

As Sister Margaret Trottier was the manager of the Community, she obtained permission to converse with Sister Le Ber, and thus speaks of the Holy Recluse: " She always evinced an ardent wish " that the buildings should be begun, assuring us " that such was God's will; and, that the Angels " would assist us. She sometimes added that, " should we not begin this year, we would not do " so later, although the necessity might be more " urgent. She spoke in such a persuasive and " inspired tone, that we immediately commenced " the work, though we possessed neither funds nor " materials."

The foundations were soon laid, and Mr. de Belmont blessed the corner stone on the 28th of May, 1713. The building was dedicated to Mary, Queen of Angels. The following inscription placed in the foundation, is a most edifying memorial of the piety and confidence that animated our heroine and the Sisters of the Congregation: " HOLY " VIRGIN, QUEEN OF ANGELS, AND REFUGE " OF MANKIND, VOUCHSAFE TO GRANT US THE " PROTECTION, WE MUST HUMBLY SOLICIT FOR " THE BEGINNING AND COMPLETION OF THIS " BUILDING, WHICH WE HAVE UNDERTAKEN IN " COMPLIANCE WITH OUR VENERABLE MOTHER'S " REQUEST. OUR MOST EARNEST DESIRE IS, " THAT WE MAY THUS CONTRIBUTE TO THE " GLORY OF THY SON, AND TO THY GREATER " HONOUR. WATCH OVER IT, IMMACULATE " VIRGIN, SO THAT MORTAL SIN MAY NEVER " ENTER BENEATH ITS ROOF. SEND GUARDIAN " SPIRITS TO PROTECT US, AND TO PROMOTE " DEVOTION TOWARDS THEE; SO THAT ALL ITS " INMATES MAY REVERE THEE, AS THEIR GUIDE, " THEIR MOTHER, AND QUEEN." Amen.

Sister Trottier adds: " Though very desirous to see the building erected, still I hesitated to undertake it, on account of our very limited resources; but no sooner did I mention my apprehensions to Sister Le Ber, than she quieted them all. She was wont to say, success would certainly crown our efforts; that she would request the Holy Angels to take charge of the undertaking, and to supply us

with all the means requisite to accomplish it. I
subsequently had reason to believe that I experienced the effects of her prayers; for I found many
unlooked for resources; moreover, I may add, that
although at liberty to have recourse to her, I seldom did so, except in cases of absolute necessity.
We had many striking proofs of the Angels' protection. The few workmen we had, were themselves often surprised at the rapid progress of their
work; from this, the report spread that they worked
during the day, and Angels during the night.
Many citizens said the same thing, and seemed
greatly surprised.

The report mentioned by Sister Trottier was not
confined to the Convent of the Congregation or to
Ville Marie: Mother Juchereau wrote from Quebec, and thus confirmed the belief, that Sister Le
Ber was assisted by Celestial Spirits. She says:
" The Holy Recluse in the execution of her em-
" broidery is assisted by Angels, with whom she is
" wont to converse, and who undoubtedly take great
" pleasure in dwelling with this Angelic being."

Sister Le Ber's confidence in the Holy Angels
and her practice of having recourse to, and of conversing with them, must have arisen from the assistance they gave her. Sister Trottier mentions a
remarkable instance of her simplicity and confidence: " She once requested me to send
" her a workman, to repair her spinning wheel: I
" forgot to do so, and shortly afterwards went to
" apologize for my negligence; adding, that I would

" atone for my fault, by immediately complying
" with her request; she smiled and said: Oh
" all is right. I had recourse to the Holy Angels,
" and they repaired my wheel; they assist me in
" all my difficulties; trust in them, and you will
" surmount all obstacles."

As soon as the building was finished, Sister Le
Ber carried out her pious design. She divested
herself of all worldly goods, to end her days in
poverty. Having collected the remainder of her
inheritance, she disposed of it on the 9th of September, 1714, to provide places in the boarding
school, for young girls in reduced circumstances.
Her intentions are thus expressed, in the Act of
donation: " Believing, that my remaining pro-
" perty could not be more suitably employed, nor
" in a manner more conformable to God's glory,
" I had determined, that the revenue it yields,
" should be henceforth devoted to the education of
" a number of young girls, whose parents cannot
" afford to give them sufficient instruction. The
" Nuns of the Congregation de Notre Dame lead
" such an edifying life, and such happy results have
" attended their efforts, that I have chosen them
" to carry out this design, trusting that my fondest
" hopes may thus be realized."

The remnant of her fortune amounted to 18,000
Canadian livres; 120 livres being the price for
boarders; the revenue of this sum would enable
the Nuns to receive seven pupils. The regulations
she drew up concerning these children's admittance

and their education, are striking proofs of her wisdom and benevolence; her desire was that none should be admitted, save those whose parents could not afford to educate them; and, that the Nuns should choose children in parishes where there were no missions of the Congregation; because such children were naturally exposed to remain ignorant all their lives; she also stipulated that orphans should be preferred; and that poor orphans of the Le Ber family should be first received.

Knowing that the Sisters of the Congregation, were called and qualified by their vocation, to educate young girls from all classes of society; that the poor and the rich receive from them, an education suitable to their position; still, she was aware that all the pupils who attend their boarding schools should not be educated in the same manner, she therefore wished that her protegées might be separated from the others, and be taught that which, their social position might hereafter require; that which a mother of a poor family should know, to earn a livelihood, and to promote her happiness. Sister Le Ber expressed her views in the following manner: " The donor wishes these young girls to " dwell as boarders in the school, and to learn what " is required to become true Christians.   Besides " Christian doctrine, they will be taught to read, " spin, knit and all sorts of useful work; to make, " wash and repair their clothes.   They will assist " in the kitchen each week, and learn housework; " by so doing, be trained to the practice of true " humility."

These regulations prove that Sister Le Ber
sought these children's welfare, and desired that
they should be spared the unhappiness attendant
on a different plan of education ; for experience
shows, that many evils resulted from the system followed in the famous Institution of Saint Cyr,
founded by royal bounty to educate young girls of
high lineage, but in reduced circumstances. The
brilliant education which they received, rendered
them unfit for the humble position they were called
to occupy in life ; and exposed them to melancholy
and unhappiness. To remove this evil, a priest of
the Seminary of Saint Sulpice, Mr. Languet de
Gergy, established a house in his parish and called
it "l'*Enfant Jesus.*" There he received noble, but
poor girls, to educate them on a plan similar to
that which Sister Le Ber chose. They were
taught all the details of housekeeping, sewing, cook-
ing, washing, ironing, and the care of a dairy ; time
has proved that this education contributed to their
happiness ; for the young ladies who left this institution, entertaining very different views from
those of the pupils of Saint Cyr, were soon enabled
to fill respectable positions in the world, thus ensuring their temporal happiness, as well as their
eternal welfare.

We mention these facts to show what a suitable
system Sister Le Ber had adopted, since a similar
one was approved throughout France.

She laid down another rule : " Writing not being
necessary for poor girls, they would incur loss of

time by devoting their attention to it.   Nevertheless, should any among them evince a desire of
embracing a religious life, they may learn to write."
Let not our readers be surprised at this regulation
of Sister Le Ber, concerning young orphan girls,
who would be obliged to earn their own livelihood :
for it proves that she not only endeavoured to promote their welfare, but also to contribute to the
good of Society.   Society at large has such multi-
plied duties to fulfil, that it needs individuals suited
to occupy different positions.   Who would accuse
Cardinal Richelieu of not having promoted public
weal, throughout France, yet, this great States-
man resolved to abolish petty Colleges, because he
thought, that far from contributing to the good of
the Country, they led most of the rising generation
to embrace high professions, when God called them
to follow mechanical pursuits ; and that social dis-
turbances were the ordinary results of such an
education.

When Sister Le Ber mentioned her rules to the
Nuns of the Congregation, Mr. de Belmont sanctioned them, and the Nuns promised not to deviate
from them, without consulting her cousin, the Baron de Longueuil, whom she had authorized to
act for her.   Mr. de Longueuil, Mr. de Belmont
and the principal Members of the Community
repaired to the apartment next to the Recluse's
cell, a Notary having read the act of donation, all
present signed it on the 9th of November, 1714.

CHAPTER IV.

SISTER LE BER'S LAST ILLNESS. HER EDIFYING
DEATH, GREAT CONCOURSE AT HER FUNERAL.

Sister Le Ber's last generous gift was the crowning act of her benevolence; and seemed to draw her nearer to eternal bliss.   It is really astonishing that both mental and bodily pain did not previously bring on death; for notwithstanding her weak constitution, she never deviated from her austere rule of life. Fasting on bread and water, macerating her flesh with various instruments of penance, lengthened prayers, constant work, interior trials, and her ardent love of God, tended to increase her mental sufferings; the thought that her heart was not filled with true charity, kept her in a state of constant anguish. The last twenty years of her life were spent amid these mortifications; still she followed all her exercices most punctually, until one night, when the cold overpowered her, while she was before the Blessed Sacrament; she was then suffering from a severe oppression which turned to pleurisy and fever. Notwithstanding her energy and fervour, she had to lay aside her usual avocations, and remain in bed; the disease progressed so rapidly, that her confessor ordered her to use sheets and a mattrass: she had not indulged in these comforts, since she had entered the Convent of the Congregation de Notre Dame.

Her intense suffering caused her no anxiety, nor did it diminish her love and solicitude for the Nuns of the Congregation; calling to mind that she had not specified who should inherit the furniture of her unpretending dwelling, she sent for a Notary, and bequeathed all that her cell contained to the Nuns of the Congregation; adding, that no one should deprive them of these articles; or any thing in their Community that had belonged to her; this act shows that she wished that the Nuns should experience no difficulty after her death; moreover she requested Mr. de Longueuil to fulfil a promise she had made to a young girl, then residing in Mississippi, by giving her 500 livres. This happened on the 22nd of September, and she signed the act, although confined to her bed.

Having thus voluntarily deprived herself of all earthly possessions, she strenuously endeavoured to prepare her soul for the great voyage, from time to eternity: those around her, then witnessed the effects of the bodily mortifications which she had practised, for such a length of time; for although, a raging fever burned within her, she never asked for any beverage to alleviate her thirst; yet, through obedience she willingly accepted what was offered her; and appeared on her bed of suffering, like a victim on the altar. She had repeated attacks of violent coughing, but respect for the Blessed Sacrament, caused her to make strenuous efforts to repress them; for she feared irreverence towards the Sacred Guest, who dwelt so near her couch; however, one morning during mass, her cough overcame her; she felt sorely grieved that this should have happened, and humbly asked pardon of God, and of all those who had heard her.

The Nuns of the Congregation became alarmed; and several wishing to see her, before her death, were accordingly admitted into her cell; she requested her attendant to answer whatever questions might be put concerning her. Her countenance all the while beamed with a serene light; her soul seemed so totally absorbed in God, that she paid but little attention to the conversation that was kept up around her.

The first day that she remained in bed, she attended to all her devotional exercises, recited long vocal prayers, and devoted the usual time to meditation; but her strength soon failed. Sister St. Charles at stated hours recited the prayers which Sister Le Ber usually said; the invalid was thus enabled to join in spirit, when extreme weakness prevented her answering them. She also sent her cousin to meditate before the Blessed Sacrament, as long as she was wont to do; and when other Nuns, came to replace Sister St. Charles, our Holy Recluse sent them likewise, both at night, and during the day, to spend the usual hours in adoration.

Two days before her death, she willed that her body should be interred in the Church of the Congregation; and, thus gave the Nuns the last proof of her affection for them, and of her confidence in their prayers. On entering her cell, she had resolved that death would not part her from those pious souls, whom she had fondly and truly loved during life, and to whom she considered herself indebted for the grace of her vocation; hence, fearing that after her decease, her relations might not comply with her request, she made a will; not to bequeath any earthly goods, for she had disposed of all, but to bind her relatives to acquiesce to her desire. The following extract contains the greater part of this edifying act: " Miss Jane Le Ber, a " recluse in the Convent of the Congregation de " Notre Dame, reflecting on the shortness of this " life, and the little time left to end her earthly " pilgrimage; having previously disposed of all the " temporal possessions which God had been pleased " to bestow upon her, has now resolved to make her " last will in the following manner :"

" In the name of the Father, and of the Son, " and of the Holy Ghost. Amen.

" Firstly, as a Christian, and a Catholic, she " recommends her soul to God, and begs Him to " admit her into His Heavenly kingdom, through the " merits of the passion, and death of His Son, Our " Lord and Saviour Jesus Christ. To obtain " eternal happiness, she solicits the intercession of " the Blessed Virgin Mary, of Saint Michael the

" Archangel, of St. John the Baptist, of the holy
" Evangelist St. John, of her holy patrons, and of
" all the Saints in Heaven."

" Secondly, she wills that after death, her body
" shall be interred next to that of her father, in the
" chapel belonging to the aforesaid Nuns of the
" Congregation de Notre Dame. This will be
" done according to the directions given by Mr.
" Charles Lemoyne, Baron of Longueuil; for, she
" has appointed him executor of this Will, and
" desires that he will faithfully fulfil all her re-
" quests."

Sister Le Ber dictated this Will during the
afternoon on the 1st of October, and though disease
had rendered her very feeble, she mustered sufficient strength to sign the document. On the following day, her fervour led her to think that she
might recite some of her usual prayers; she therefore asked for a book, to say the office of the
Cross; her attendant raised her to a sitting posture,
and placed the book in her hands; but the invalid
was scarcely seated, when a sudden dizziness came
over her; and such entire prostration followed, that
all present thought her end was near, and that she
should consequently receive the Holy Viaticum.
The Blessed Sacrament was conveyed to her chamber, in the most solemn manner. All the Nuns
accompanied it, carrying lighted tapers, as far as
her cell; a few entered, and witnessed this touching ceremony. This happened on the 2nd of October, the day devoted to honor the Holy Angels, in

whom she had always placed such implicit trust. We may naturally suppose that her unceasing endeavours to imitate these happy spirits, induced them to reward her piety, by hovering around her death bed, while terrestrial angels ministered to her corporal wants. Words can ill express her feelings, at that solemn moment; her whole life proved, that nought, but religious respect, and ardent love for Jesus Christ, truly present in the Blessed Sacrament, had induced her to choose a retired life, and to persevere unremittingly in it. As death drew nearer, a heavenly light illuminated her countenance, and seemed to indicate that she had united all her acts of profound religion, of ardent love and of unbounded confidence to offer them to her Divine Spouse as the most pleasing homage, He could receive, and the last act of a life which had been wholly consecrated to Him. Her sufferings and the care she required were little thought of, when Our Lord had entered her heart: her happiness engrossed her entire attention; she requested that her bed curtains should be closed, so that no earthly thought might disturb her, and that she might give vent to her ardent feelings.

Thus she spent the remainder of the day, confiding her soul to her Heavenly Father's care, and willingly immolating her life, for God's greater glory; nought but sudden transports of love disturbed her wonted calmness. Her heart yearned for the blissful moment, which was to unite her to her Spouse; but, all this time, life was waning, she felt it, and requested that Extreme Unction should be administered. She was therefore anointed at about 2 o'clock in the morning, then fell into a quiet agony, during which all present joined in the usual prayers for the agonizing. Death finally relieved her captive soul; she expired at 9 o'clock A. M. on the 3rd of October, 1714, so tranquilly and yet so joyfully, that it seemed, as if she had enjoyed a fore-shadowing of eternal bliss. She was fifty-two years and nine months old. Her edifying death produced deep and lasting impressions on the Sisters of the Congregation; we may even add that it created an atmosphere of sanctity around them; and also wrought happy results throughout the town, and the country parishes. As soon as Sister Le Ber departed this life, the Nuns hastened to testify their veneration for one, whom the entire Community had respected. Their first care was to clothe her in her usual garments, in order to satisfy their own devotion, and that of the faithful, by laying her out in the Church; but her dress was so old and worn, that they were obliged to make another, before placing her in her coffin. Death did not give her countenance that repulsive appearance it so often imparts; her features beamed with that expression of candour, modesty, and in-nocence which had characterized her during life; no one wearied gazing on her Angelic face, and all sighed for the happiness which they felt confident she must enjoy.

Her corpse was exposed during two days, to

satisfy the praiseworthy devotion and curiosity, which induced so many to witness this novel scene ; the whole city was astir. All the citizens assembled to venerate the mortal remains of one, whom many amongst them had never seen, though she had lived and died in their midst.

A high opinion of her sanctity, and confidence in her prayers, prompted many to lay rosaries, and other objects of devotion, on her body. This holy Recluse's death excited so much interest, that news of it spread throughout the country. Mother Juchereau from her cloister in the General Hospital of Quebec, alludes to it in the following manner: " Sister Le Ber was exposed in the Church of the " Congregation de Notre Dame, her face uncovered, " and remained so, during two days for the conso- " lation, and edification of the faithful of Montreal, " and its environs: crowds came to behold the " remains of this Holy Virgin. Her tattered gar- " ments, and even her old straw shoes were distri- " buted among the people; those who obtained " anything that had belonged to her, considered it " a relic, and returned delighted. It is affirmed " that persons suffering from various diseases were " cured on touching her coffin, with respect and " faith. The people's devotion being satisfied, her " magnificent obsequies followed. The corpse was " brought to the Parish Church, a solemn funeral " service was sung, and Mr. de Belmont, Superior " of the Seminary of Saint Sulpice, and Vicar " General, pronounced a touching panegyric on the

" departed Recluse. Her remains were subsequent-
" ly conveyed to the Church of the Congregation
" of Notre Dame, and interred next to those of her
" father."

Respect for her whose mortal remains they
possessed, and gratitude for the many gifts she had
bestowed upon their Institution, induced the Nuns
to have the following inscription, written in golden
letters, placed on her tomb :

HERE LIES THE VENERABLE SISTER JANE LE
BER, A BENEFACTRESS OF THIS INSTITUTION.
HAVING LED A RETIRED LIFE, DURING FIF-
TEEN YEARS IN HER OWN HOME, SHE WITH-
DREW TO THIS CONVENT, AND IN THIS RETREAT
PASSED THE LAST TWENTY YEARS OF HER LIFE.
SHE DEPARTED THIS LIFE IN THE 53RD YEAR
OF HER AGE ON THE 3RD OF OCTOBER 1714.

In 1721, Mr. de Belmont wrote an abridgment
of Sister Le Ber's life and dedicated it to Mr.
Maurice Le Pelletier, director of the Seminary of
St. Sulpice in Paris: he thus mentioned the veneration in which she was held: " Many Novenas
" and secret prayers are offered upon Sister Le
" Ber's tomb ; several persons acknowledge that
" they have obtained cures through her interces-
" sion. All consider her as a Saint, and designate
" her as such."

CHAPTER V.

The funeral oration which Mr. de Belmont delivered on Sister Le Ber, the day of her obsequies, is the most suitable conclusion to this edifying life; this eulogium proves the high opinion all had of this holy Virgin's sanctity. Being addressed to the citizens of Ville Marie, and delivered over the remains of the deceased, it was a public and solemn acknowledgment, of Divine Providence in Sister Le Ber's vocation; and also tended to prove, what we asserted in the Introduction to this life, that God had chosen this Holy Recluse, to renew the fervour and virtues of the solitaries of the primitive ages; and to awaken feelings of holy emulation within many a young heart. Mr. de Belmont called to mind the Divine Wisdom manifested in this favoured soul's vocation; he alluded to the manifold blessings and favours, her prayers had obtained for her country; and comparing her to Judith, he fearlessly applied to our Canadian

heroine, those words which greeted the liberatrix
of Bethulia.

" *Tu honorificentia populi nostri.*"

" You are the honor of our people."

" Sisters, our prayers have been offered up for
" the Illustrious Virgin, whose loss we so keenly feel;
" but gratitude requires that a public testimonial
" should honor her, who increased, the Church's
" glory, and her country's weal. Her examples of
" virtue have found an echo within many hearts;
" they have drawn down the favours of the most
" High on numerous souls, and many a Christian
" Virgin here present, is indebted to Sister Le Ber
" for her calling. That Holy Recluse's prayers
" shielded us from wars and plagues; and it is our
" bounden duty to hail her advent to the world of
" bliss, with the note of praise, and the song of
" triumph. Gentlemen, this Holy Recluse's edify-
" ing and extraordinary life is an honor to our
" city; it will encircle our age with the bright halo
" which illumined the history of the first centuries
" of the Church; and the New World will thus
" acquire pre-eminence over the homes of our fore-
" fathers; for I can safely say, that the whole of
" Christendom can scarcely boast of another such
" Angelic being, as this young girl, who faithfully
" reproduced the virtues which the most austere
" anchorites practiced. This corrupt age is desti-
" tute of such heroism."

" Entire reclusion is the most striking feature in

" her existence, and should first elicit our admir-
" ation; let us then dwell on this alone, and com-
" pare it to that which ancient solitaries embraced;
" let us, for a moment, forget her spotless purity,
" and childlike innocence; her humble devotion,
" and sublime contemplation ; her forgetfulness of
" self and benevolence towards others; to meditate
" solely, on that solitude, which rendered her the
" wonder of our age, and elevated her to such a
" high degree of sanctity, that miraculous inter-
" vention would be required to enable others to
" imitate her. Man is by nature a social being ;
" hence, a solitary life has always been considered as
" the greatest triumph of grace over nature, and
" the summit of Christian perfection. Read the
" lives of the Fathers of the desert ; there you will
" see, Anchorits compared to sublime Angels, who
" unceasingly chant the praises of the Almighty ;
" or, to Enoch and Elias dwelling in an ethereal
" region, free from vicissitudes, and whose exist-
" ence is one continued contemplation. Some au-
" thors have even compared them to those bright
" luminaries that adorn the firmament, but at such
" a distance from earth, that our knowledge of them,
" is founded merely on the influence they exert
" over us."

" Such then was the sublime life, our illustrious
" recluse was called to. To prove her heroism, we
" shall draw a comparison between her, and world-
" renowned solitaries; rock and thicket need nei-
" ther impede our course nor baffle our researches.

" Ask him who has assumed the hermit's garb,
" why he lives isolated from the world ; his answer
" is, that the bright days of his youth were spent
" in sin and forgetfulness of God—he has sought
" the forest's depths, to atone for many years of
" crime. Our Holy Recluse entered her cell with a
" heart as pure and spotless as the babe on whose
" brow, the regenerating waters of Baptism, still
" glisten ; she followed the Lamb into the closed
" garden, still retaining the spotless garb His blood
" had purified ; purity shone upon her brow, and
" fairest lilies bloomed around her, for earth had
" never breathed upon them, nor had passion
" polluted them. History seldom mentions young
" girls who dwelt in solitude, and though it should
" allude to some, like a Magdalen, a Mary of Egypt
" dwelling in the darkest forests, it also informs
" us that this was in atonement for past crimes—
" here we behold a follower of the loving Magdalen
" fondly pursuing Jesus' steps, and sipping the
" inebriating nectar of His life-giving words, but
" not of worldly Magdalen, seeking earth's transient
" joys and pleasures. Here, also can we admire
" that of which antiquity can seldom boast ; the rare
" union of mortification and of innocence, of spiri-
" tual fortitude and of bodily weakness."

" Let us follow up the comparison until the pre-
" sent age, and remark the characteristic features
" of our Recluse's mode of live. Trappists, Car-
" thusians dwell in retirement, yet, they daily
" meet in the sacred abode of the Most High, and

" unite in hymns of praise and love—Exercise and
" manual labour, fatiguing though they may be,
" are some relaxation from a continued mental
" strain; but our solitary dwelt in a narrow cham-
" ber, and refused herself the satisfaction of even
" contemplating the firmament. History informs
" us that a fervent hermit had willingly chained,
" himself in a small space; and his Bishop gave
" orders for his liberation. Still had he remained
" in his voluntary prison, he could at least have
" looked upon the sky; while nought but the walls
" of a cell, ever greeted Sister Le Ber's gaze. Per-
" severance may be truly termed heroic, when it
" leads human nature, to accomplish such acts; but
" it would inflict insupportable torments if a long-
" ing for eternity, a steadfast belief in happiness
" beyond the grave, did not amply compensate a
" soul for all these sacrifices. Our solitary yearned
" for the happy day, which would unite her to her
" Heavenly Spouse. John the Baptist was her
" patron, and her model; like him, she closed her
" eyes on earth's greatest treasures, to gaze solely
" on her loving Lord and Master."

" The most austere solitaries spoke of God's mercy
" and of his works, whilst you, thrice blessed soul !
" never gave vent to your feelings, and seemed to
" dread the use of language. When you expressed
" your thoughts, it was in a lowly spirit, as Jesus
" did in Nazareth. From your childhood you sought
" to imitate Mary's interior communications with
" God, and the last twenty years of your existence

" were a faithful representation of Christ's death
." and burial. This perpetual silence is undoubted-
" ly the acknowledged feature of the strong
" minded woman, but where find her? Shall we
" go to distant lands? Gentlemen, our own city
" has produced her. Yes, this holy Recluse's life
" was one continued miracle, and the Almighty
" chose our infant Church, and virgin soil, solely,
" for its accomplishment; unless, through a second
" miracle, he renews this prodigy in some other
" favoured soul called to walk in her footsteps.
" But, alas! what hopes can we entertain, that this
" will be realized."

" We must not however bestow fruitless admira-
" tion on this holy Virgin: her sublime virtues,
" though far above ordinary merit, can surely give
" rise to happier results; for, though she endeavour-
" ed to lead a hidden life, and even sought to bury
" herself alive, some bright rays have shone through
" this voluntary obscurity. We can now enter the
" holy abode in which she dwelt for a number of
" years; and interrogate those walls, sole witness
" of her Angelic life; therein, do we behold traces
" of virtues, that all can imitate; antidotes to
" vice, and means to overcome it."

" Her devotion to the Blessed Sacrament, her
" profound religion, and the ardent zeal that led her
" to decorate Christ's earthly dwelling; her faith-
" ful imitation of the life the Blessed Virgin led
" during her stay in the Temple, her devotion to
" the Holy Angels, and her endeavours to imitate

" them by continual prayer. There also do we
" learn, her love of poverty and of Christ's suffer-
" ing members ; her humility and simplicity ; and
" if, we would fain acquire fuller information, let
" us ask it of Jesus in His Sacrament of love, of
" Mary her protectress, and of the Angelic spirits,
" who willingly hovered round her ; else, we must
" needs indulge in suppositions, for her humility
" has drawn an impenetrable veil over her mani-
" fold virtues."

" We are aware that her cell was so constructed
" as to place her couch, in close proximity to the
" Blessed Sacrament ; four inches only, intervened
" between her dwelling, and that of her heart's
" Beloved ; she thus nightly enjoyed the privilege
" once granted to the Beloved Disciple, when he
" rested on His Saviour's bosom. What heavenly
" communications must she not have received,
" when her heart found life and light in Him, who
" illumines the universe, He must have said to her,
" as He had said to Jacob : *This land, where you
" rest, will one day be your inheritance.*"

" Gentlemen, we may here give free scope to
" our imagination ; still, it will never fathom the
" depth of the love outpoured in these sweet com-
" munications."

" O Jesus ! concealed beneath the Sacramental
" veils, be thou our guide, and our instructor ; tell
" us what passed between thee and thy chosen
" spouse. Didst thou not charm her ear, with the
" most delightful strains ? . . . Did not thy voice

" penetrate the slight partition, and articulate those
" words of the Canticle of Canticles : *Open to me,*
" *my Sister, my spouse, open to me ?*   How often
" on awaking from her sleep did she not say within
" herself : *Behold He standeth behind our wall*
" *looking through the windows, looking through*
" *the lattices.   I sleep, and my heart watches.*
" O Heavenly communications !   Created love,
" how empty are other joys compared to thy celes-
" tial delights.   But why defile this hallowed in-
" tercourse by using feeble terms to magnify that
" which we never can comprehend !   Angelic Spi-
" rits, have ye not witnessed these out-pourings
" with rapturous admiration ?   Did thoughts of
" sacred emulation not arise within thy minds ?
" But these comparisons merely tend to diminish
" the glory of those actions, which will one day be
" revealed to the world, with undimmed splendour.
" We can now revert to well-known facts : she fol-
" lowed the custom adopted by the Franciscans and
" other austere religious orders.   She arose every
" night and spent an hour on her knees, in silent
" adoration before the Blessed Sacrament.   While
" darkness reigned, and all were wrapped in slum-
" bers, rendering no homage to the Most High ; this
" incomparable Virgin stood forth, as the Church's
" advocate, and her country's shield.   During twen-
" ty years, Canada's frosts never caused her to give
" up this act of devotion ; still they were keenly felt
" by her whose emaciated body had been victim to
" so many penitential practices. *O, Jesus, lover*

" *of crucified souls!* thou wert pleased to choose
" this pious practice to be the instrument of thy
" spouse's martyrdom: death met her, in those
" protracted night meditations. Thou didst im-
" molate her on the altar-step as a victim of thanks-
" giving, which Thou thyself hadst chosen. Dur-
" ing twenty years, she burned before Thy Ta-
" bernacle like a bright lamp: Thou hast now
" extinguished the light which emanated from her
" mortal heart, to enkindle new flames in her
" beatified spirit, and make it shine forth as a
" brilliant luminary whose beneficient rays will
" illumine this Church."

" We should here mention the numerous morti-
" fications her ardent love induced her to practice;
" but, who can unfold those secrets; who can tell
" us, how she macerated her innocent body ? . . .
" the silent walls of Her cell were the sole witness
" of all. O Virgin, ever blessed mother of Jesus,
" model of all holy souls, since none can be sanc-
" tified save by copying thee, thy Divine Son's
" most perfect worshipper; tell us wherein Jane
" Le Ber most resembled thee ! . . . Thou didst
" seek solitude beneath the Temple's shade, and
" during twelve years, thou alone among the
" daughters of Juda, didst enjoy the privilege of
" entering the Holy of Holies."

" Our Recluse spent the last twenty years of
" her existence, in a dwelling laid out like thine
" own apartment now called the *Holy chamber;*
" she thus dwelt in the immediate vicinity of Him,

" who is the true *Holy of Holies*. It was in this
" cell, that thy faithful daughter followed thy
" example, that she too made garments for Jesus,
" by preparing the linen destined for the altar, and
" vestments for His Ministers. Thou wert the
" Instructress, and she the docile novice; thou
" didst guide her taste, and direct her needle,
" while she embroidered the costly vestment we
" now admire; thou didst teach her to blend gold
" and silver, to rival nature's works, and to inspire
" others with a desire of adoring thy Son's dwell-
" ing among us."

You, Heavenly Spirits, who fondly gazed on this
" pure maiden in whom you beheld not earth's
" corruption, but a mind almost as pure as your
" own ; therefore surrounding her with sweet fami-
" liarity, make known to us, the treasures she
" acquired while conversing with you."

" Was not heavenly wisdom the reward she ob-
" tained ? Was not her soul imbued with this
" fundamental truth, *God in all, he who posses-*
" *ses Him, has the fulness of all felicity ; and who*
" *knows Him not, is in the most abject poverty.*
" Next to God, *the only true riches are spiritual*
" *favours, salvation, and eternity.*"

" She must also have learned that the intelligent'
" immortal substance, that emanation from the
" Divinity, which we call soul, is our only treasure ;
" that to save it no pains can be too great, no dif-
" ficulties insurmountable ; that an insatiable love
" of riches, of honors and pleasures is the soul's

" greatest enemy, on account of its tendency to
" degrade and corrupt this spiritual part of our
" nature; and to impart inclinations, that defile it
" during life, and give rise to despair when it is
" about to appear before the Sovereign Judge."

" Such then were the happy results of her me-
" ditations, or rather of her uninterrupted commu-
" nications with Angelic Spirits."

" The Almighty had endowed her with the goods
" of this earth, but she renounced all, to die in
" poverty; or, rather to ensure the possession of
" imperishable treasures. Her work adorns every
" altar. Every Parish possesses some specimen of
" her artistic genius, we never can weary admiring
" her laborious assiduity, and the love of poverty
" displayed in her clothing; wearing coarse straw
" shoes; and such tattered garments that after her
" death others had to be made, to lay her out. All
" this was done to practice that profound humility,
" which rendered Canada's wealthiest heiress, the
" most destitute maiden in the country. Even had
" sufficient time elapsed since her death to enable
" us to expatiate more at length on her merit, this
" humility would conceal all from our gaze, as it
" concealed her manifold virtues, from those who
" beheld her during life. Heroic silence.!.... thou
" didst extinguish this brilliant luminary, or,
" rather thou didst screen it from mortal eyes. St.
" Bernard tell us that this self same silence, would
" be an advantage to preachers themselves, whose

N

" sanctity is often dimmed by vain glory, human
" respect, and love of applause."

" Daughters of Ville Marie, will *despair* of ever
" imitating this saintly Virgin, be the only result
" of the recital of her heroic life ? Why despair ?
" Did she not dwell in your midst, and inhale the
" air you daily breathe ? Will the contrast be-
" tween her fervour and your indifference, merely
" give rise to the following thought : *Sister Le Ber*
" *was a Saint, but I belong to the world and have*
" *no pretentions to her sanctity ; such is not my lot.*"

" Stay at least, for one moment, the worldly
" current of your thoughts, reflect on the numerous
" dangers from which solitude delivered her, and
" view the fearful loss, you incur by voluntarily
" condemning yourselves to your present manner
" of living.   She mortified her body, and reduced
" all her senses to subjection.   She closed her eyes
" on worldly objects, your looks wound many a
" heart, and kindle many an unhallowed flame.
" Your immodest dresses are snares set for pure
" minds, and new occasions of sin, for those whom
" Satan has already conquered."

" That thorny diadem which rested on the Re-
" deemer's brow, seems to have guarded her hear-
" ing, and banished all frivolous discourses ; but
" you, daughters of the world, revel in vain delights,
" in deceptive flattery, and in the insinuating lan-
" guage of worldlings. Your hearing is an ever-open
" path, wherein sin glides with all its abomination ;
" although, the wily serpent is sometimes concealed

" by flowers imprudent words never passed her lips;
" her tongue was bound down to perpetual silence ;
" and yours is often instrumental in wounding
" charity. She voluntarily condemned herself to
" entire reclusion, and you yearn for the moment,
" when liberty will be granted you, and enable you
" to wander with inclination for your sole guide.
" Why forget this important truth, that ignorance
" of the world and of its false maxims is innocence's
" surest shield! ... *Children of men, how long*
" *will you persist, in seeking deceit and vanity ?*"

" A feeling of horror difficult to express, is ex-
" perienced on witnessing a licentious person's
" deathbed. Hell's fire seems to burn around, and
" the infernal spirits endeavour to rob the passive
" tomb, in order to hasten the beginning of their
" victim's tortures; but all fear is banished, when
" a Saint dies, for her death excites feelings of love,
" of confidence and of devotion. Heaven's light
" seems reflected on her countenance, and Angels
" hover round her corpse. You have witnessed this
" spectacle, in the incomparable Virgin who lately
" expired."

" Mothers and daughters of Ville Marie, she is
" your model, she it is, whom you should imitate.
" But say you, my aim is not to be canonized.
" Yet God requires that all should be sanctified in
" their various states of life, and on the last day
" will not the virtues of Canada's heroine rise in
" judgment against you."

" Let me not however intermingle threats with

" praises. Yes, soul of grace, be thou our advo-
" cate. Holy Recluse whom my heart invokes, and
" whom I would fain salute as a Saint, did the
" Church allow it; we mourn over our past negli-
" gence, we dread the contrast between thy fervour,
" and our indifference; may the Almighty render
" us thy imitators on earth, as we hope to be
" partakers of thy glory in Heaven."

" Amen."

PILGRIMAGE

TO THE CHURCH OF THE CONGREGATION DE NOTRE DAME, WHERE SISTER LE BER DWELT AS A RECLUSE AND WHEREIN HER REMAINS WERE INTERRED.

After Sister Le Ber's death, her apartments, and the little furniture they contained were considered as precious relics. Those of her fellow citizens who repaired to her tomb, to reclaim the assistance of her prayers, also visited her cell with feelings of respect and veneration; for to them, it was a memorial of the heroic virtues she had so zealously practised. In 1768 the buildings of the Congregation having been destroyed by fire, no trace of Sister Le Ber's cell was left: a new Church was afterwards raised on the foundations of the old; the space formerly occupied by the Recluse's cell, was added to the Church, and subsequently became its sanctuary.

The increase of population in Ville Marie, induced the Sisters of the Congregation de Notre

Dame to erect a third, and larger one : their praise-worthy design, has been most successfully carried out; but, to realize it, they had to suffer many privations. At the present day, a beautiful Church in the Grecian Style of architecture, stands on the same spot, where Sister Le Ber and Sister Bour-geoys erected the first Church of the Congregation ; which extended from the entrance, to the centre, of that just completed.

A Monument on the right, marks the spot where the holy Recluse's remains are deposited : When her coffin was opened in 1822, it was found to contain a heap of dust : this entire dissolution was attributed to Sister Le Ber's delicate constitu-tion, and austere mode of living.

Thus, the centre of the new Church, is the favoured spot, where Miss Le Ber spent the last twenty years of her life. There, she dwelt as a public victim, offering herself daily, in sacrifice to God, to obtain Heaven's choicest blessings, on her fellow citizens, desiring above all, the sanctification of youth.

As this cell had been her only dwelling from the moment of her seclusion, may we not hope, that though her spirit inhabits the blessed realms above, it also hovers around this new sanctuary ; and as she now freely draws from the true fountain of pure love, she will continue that mission of zeal and charity, begun during her childhood, and continued until her death ?

Very few among us are called to imitate her

entire seclusion, that heavenly life which brought her in such close commune with Angelic Spirits; yet, all Christians, eager to procure God's glory, can, and should, endeavour to imitate her zeal for the salvation of souls, and her indefatigable efforts to bring them to their Creator. May we not indulge in the belief, that her fondest wishes are gratified when she beholds fervent Catholics, repair to this new Church, and there offer prayers for themselves, and for their country? And are we not naturally led to suppose, that her supplications are united to theirs? so that this same spot, will, from age to age, re-echo with the prayers of those, whom we may consider as worthy heirs of her zeal?

The Almighty has evidently been pleased to choose the new Church for this purpose. This Sanctuary is doubly hallowed as the dwelling of the sainted soul, who offered herself to God as a public victim; and as a new pilgrimage, dedicated to Mary, refuge of Sinners. All are called thither, sinners, to obtain forgiveness of their sins; and the just, to draw upon themselves and others, the abundant graces obtained through the intercession of that Immaculate Virgin, who is the dispenser of Heavenly favors.

Our munificent Father has willed that this sanctuary should be enriched with a miraculous statue, honored during five or six Centuries in France, as having been the instrument of numerous cures, and other blessings. This holy object attracts crowds, who daily assemble to witness new proofs of God's goodness.

Time had weakened recollections of Sister Le Ber; her austere life, and heroic virtues found few imitators; and might have failed to attract the faithful towards this spot; hence, God was pleased to draw them thither, with hopes of promoting their own welfare. The decrees of Divine Wisdom have been fulfilled, ever since the miraculous statue has become the property of the Nuns of the Congregation de Notre Dame.

As soon as this object of general veneration arrived in Canada, many pious souls were led to implore the assistance of the Mother of Sorrows, and to pray before the holy statue, whereby Mary's excessive love for man is so ably portrayed. Those who venerated this statue before its removal to this country always asked for some of the oil which burned before it; this, they applied to the sick: and God frequently rewarded their confidence in Mary's intercession. The first who venerated this statue after its arrival in Ville Marie, requested the Nuns to let them have a little of the oil from the lamps placed before the image of the Mother of Sorrow. Does this fact not prove that Canada is destined to witness a renewal of the Miracles previously wrought in France? For neither the Nuns, nor the faithful had ever heard that this custom hitherto existed. The implicit trust thereby manifested has been amply rewarded; wonderful cures are not confined to Ville Marie; many have taken place throughout Canada; and the faithful from neighboring Parishes possess no more precious treasure, than a few drops of the oil from this Lamp.

These corporal cures are not however the choicest blessings which the Almighty has in store. He cured bodily ailments to win the confidence of His Creatures, and thereby deliver them from sin, the only true evil. Sister Le Ber sought no other end in condemning herself to perpetual solitude. This ardent desire of banishing sin from the heart of man induced the Son of God to become Incarnate, and Mary to consent to the immolation of her Divine Son. The crimes of mankind then arose before Her; in them She beheld Her Divine Son's executioners, Jesus' lifeless body lay torn and mangled in Her arms, 'a heart-rending spectacle to a Mother's eye ; yet, manifold offenses caused the bitterest tears to flow; filled Her soul with unutterable anguish; and formed the Sword of Sorrow that pierced Her Heart. She wept over Sinners in weeping over the crucified body of Jesus, Victim of their crimes. This afflicted Mother took upon Herself the burden of Her Children's sins, she mourned over them as if she alone had been guilty, and finally offered Herself to the Justice of the Most High as a victim, on whom He might inflict the chastisements deserved by sinful man. Mary's only design is, that sinners' hearts may be moved by that feeling of sincere contrition which filled Her own. This would be the most solid, the most desirable and the most salutary result which devotion to our Lady of Pity could produce; and a desire of obtaining it raised Sister Le Ber to that sanctity and degree of Perfection for which she is famed; and ensured her the endless happiness she now enjoys in Heaven.

TABLE OF CONTENTS.

BOOK SECOND.

Miss Le Ber's sojourn in her family, from her departure from School until her withdrawal into the Convent of the Congregation de Notre Dame.

BOOK THIRD.

Miss Le Ber enters the Convent of the Congregation de Notre Dame. Her love and devotion towards the Blessed Sacrament.

BOOK FOURTH

Sister Le Ber's devotion to the Blessed Virgin. Her affection for the Congregation de Notre Dame. Her holy death.